COAL

a cautionary christmas ✷ tale ✷

by Chris Savino

Dedicated to:
Good little children, everywhere.
(and the naughty ones, too)

This plan worked quite well and lasted for many years, but all that changed the Christmas Charlie was eleven.

Outside, snow blew in dizzying array, causing bare branches to bat against the window of the Peters' home. Inside, the scent of pine needles and fresh baked cookies mingled in the air. The Christmas tree's alternating multi-colored lights danced over glassy ornaments, casting splotchy shadows on the ceiling. Hand-knitted stockings hung on the mantel, each carefully stitched with an embroidered name.

Emily knelt by the coffee table, coloring a picture for Santa, and Charlie stood at the fireplace with the poker tool in hand. He stabbed at the burning logs, causing them to snap and crackle, sending embers up the chimney and out into the crisp night air.

Charlie took the poker and lifted a Santa-shaped ornament from off the tree. He held the ornament over the flames. The ornament softened, before it melted and drooped.

Charlie! Emily said.

Charlie smirked. When the ornament was sufficiently melted into a contorted mess worthy of a nightmare, he pulled it from the flame. He blew on the melted blob, smiling, and then hung it back onto the tree.

Emily watched, speechless.

"Santa can see you, ya know," she finally said. "He knows when you've been bad or good."

"Yeah, yeah. Big deal," Charlie responded. "It's Christmas Eve. I'm already getting presents."

Emily's cheeks flushed. "That isn't how it works. Santa *knows*."

"Oh, yeah? What is he? Magic?"

"No... he's just... Santa Claus."

Charlie scoffed.

The firelight illuminated Emily's golden hair. "If you're not good, you're *not* going to get presents."

"And how do you know? Did one of his *little elves* tell you?"

"Charlie! I'm being serious!"

He scoffed again.

"You're going to get a lump of coal in your stocking."

Charlie crossed his arms. "The presents will be under the tree in just a few short hours and *nothing* will change that."

Emily bit her lips and wiped her nose. "I wish you'd just be nice, Charlie."

"I am nice." He smiled.

"Only when you want presents. Why can't you be nice all the

time?"

"Where's the fun in that?"

"Emily?" their mother called from the kitchen. "Will you help me frost these cookies?"

"Don't worry," Charlie said. "I'll finish decorating the tree." He picked off another ornament with the poker. He grinned his usual up-to-no-good grin.

Emily stared at her brother.

"Why won't you just be good?" she whispered. "I want you to be good."

She set her crayon down, and marched from the room.

Charlie glared after her as she exited the room, his shoulders slumping. His mouth went dry and he wiped his nose. He hated that he was so mean, but he couldn't help it—it was just the way he was.

He glanced down at the coffee table and noticed the picture Emily had drawn of the North Pole. Glittering elves danced around Santa and his sack full of gifts. Snow sparkled around the scene, each snowflake a different size and pattern. Santa's rosy cheeks mirrored his sleek, red sleigh, each of his reindeer smiling and ready to take flight into the clear, starry night.

Charlie tightened his grip on the poker, before he dropped it and stomped over to the coffee table. He parked himself down, grabbed the crayons, and scribbled over her artwork.

He drew large horns curling out from Santa's head, and pointy teeth on each of the elves. Instead of magical reindeer, he made them grotesque man-beasts, large enough to cover the sparkling snow. He took his fingernail and scraped off the glitter that Emily had strategically glued onto each snowflake. He then blackened out the elves and gifts, making them look dirty, stained, and grimy.

Charlie's mouth quirked up to the side.

Here's what Santa and his evil minions really look like.

The wind howled outside, and dishes clanked in the kitchen. Shadows from the fire flickered on the walls. Charlie held up his masterpiece, and the flames casted an eerie glow through the paper.

With a gleam in his eye, his mouth spread into a slow, mischievous smile.

He couldn't help it. It was just the way he was.

2.

The Stockings were hung by the chimney with care...

Charlie tapped his fingers, staring at the kitchen clock. Only a few more hours until Christmas morning. Water ran from the faucet as his mother scrubbed the dishes, and his father stood next to her, drying them. Charlie kicked his legs underneath the kitchen table, and he let out a loud breath. He could swear the hands on the clock were going backwards. Would this night never end?

Emily sat across from him, squeezing white frosting from a tube onto a man-shaped cookie. She picked up a few silver sprinkles and placed them onto the little man, making buttons down the front of him. Her face lit up as she carefully set him on a white and gold candy cane plate.

"There," she said. "He's all ready for Santa. I hope he likes it!"

Charlie reached over and plucked up the cookie. Making his voice high and waving the little man in the air he said, "No, don't eat me! I've lived a good life!"

"Charlie, give it back!" Emily cried.

She tried to retrieve the cookie, but Charlie swatted her hand away. He opened his mouth, and slowly moved the cookie toward it.

"Charlie! Don't!"

He inched the man closer. "No, please. I've got a wife and children!"

"Mom!"

Charlie smirked, bit off its head and quickly chewed.

"Blech!" Charlie said, spitting out the brown, gooey mess onto the table. He scraped the remaining cookie off his tongue and then wiped his fingers on his black t-shirt. He'd ruined his favorite color. "Gingerbread? Why does it always have to be gingerbread? I hate gingerbread. Ugh!"

Emily lifted her chin and pressed her lips together. "Now I have to start all over!"

The faucet turned off, and Charlie's mother spun around. She set her hands on her hips. "You're going to help your sister finish decorating those cookies," she said. "And if I hear one more squabble, then you're going to bed early."

His parents left the room, and Charlie listened as their footsteps

10

marched upstairs.

"Here you go," Emily whispered. She slid the plate of fresh, undecorated gingerbread over to Charlie. "You can have the good ones."

Charlie rolled his eyes.

Tiny pellets of snow started to pelt the windows as the wind whipped outside. Carolers sung down the street, before they disappeared, their voices swallowed up in the storm.

Charlie put his chin in his hands and checked the clock again.

All Charlie could think about was the loot he would get tomorrow morning. He shut his eyes and imagined his fingers ripping into the wrapped gifts tucked neatly under the tree, revealing a Laser Blaster. A magic kit. A robotic hand. Slime ball prank set. Telescope. Snowboard. And of course, the new Navy Seal action figure with interchangeable combat gear and Kung fu grip.

He'd been extra nice the past two weeks for that one.

Charlie grinned at his cleverness.

Once again, his scheme of being *just good enough* before Christmas had worked.

"Are you finished?" Emily asked. "Charlie?"

Charlie jerked out of his daydream. "What?"

"Your gingerbread man. Are you finished decorating?"

Charlie snatched a cookie from the plate, grabbed the tube, and squirted out a green glob, mushing the frosting everywhere. "Done."

Emily sighed, reached over and picked up the green goopy mess. She held the cookie in both hands, her eyebrows creased, before they shot upward. "Wow, good job, Charlie! It looks just like the Grinch. Santa will love it!" She placed it next to the angel gingerbread man she made on the plate. She straightened the two cookies so it looked like they were holding hands.

Charlie snorted.

Emily skipped to the fridge, took out a tall glass of chilled milk, and motioned to Charlie. "Come on! We've got to set these out by the fireplace for Santa!"

Charlie trudged after her, groaning. He didn't like these pointless traditions. It was kiddie stuff, and he was eleven years old. He hadn't believed in Santa since he was five. Same with reindeer, elves, a flying sleigh, or a magical North Pole. But if faking it through these dumb traditions got him one step closer to Christmas morning, it was worth it. He just needed to get through the night.

Fluffy was curled up by the fire when Charlie and Emily walked in. The cat, still missing the fur on her tail from the time Charlie had experimented on it with his Chemistry set—made her look like an opossum.

Fluffy peeked an eye open, took one look at Charlie, and hissed, scurrying from the room.

As Emily set down the milk and cookies on the end table nearest the fireplace, she screamed.

Charlie jerked.

"*What* have you done to my picture?" She shoved the paper in his face.

Charlie blinked, and his vision came into focus.

"Oh," Charlie said with a little bit of pride in his voice, "I fixed it."

"No! You ruined it! Why do my reindeer look like gross horse men?"

"Those are Minotaurs, thank you very much."

"And what did you do to my elves? Why is one nibbling on Santa's toes?"

"Because that's what elves like to do, duhhh."

"And… and… and…" Her voice cracked. "And why does Santa

13

have... *horns*?"

Charlie's mouth lifted at the corners. "Oh, that's not Santa Claus, it's Krampus."

Emily's lip quivered. She stared at her brother with her wide eyes, tears glistening in the corners. The fire crackled behind her, elongating her shadow on the wall.

"You're going to get coal in your stocking tomorrow morning," she whispered. "And I'm not even sure if I'll be sad or not."

Footsteps thumped from upstairs. Charlie's mother rushed down the staircase.

"Charlie? What did you do?"

Emily slowly hid the drawing behind her back.

"Why do you always think it's me?"

"Because it is always you."

"You are not wrong," Charlie admitted.

His mother narrowed her eyes. Her sharp fingernail pointed upstairs.

"Up," she said to Charlie. "To bed. I warned you. Now you don't get to listen to your father read *'Twas a Night Before Christmas*."

Charlie glared back at Emily before stomping upstairs.

14

With his teeth brushed, and his blue and white striped pajama bottoms on, Charlie plunked down onto his bed. The foam mattress sunk downward, his head pressing into the feathered pillow.

Charlie stared up at the ceiling, his hands behind his head. Emily's voice resounded in his mind. *Coal in your stocking.* Ridiculous. Even if Santa existed, where would he get all of his coal? It's not like he had a coal mine at the North Pole. He snorted at the mere thought.

Muffled voices drifted from Emily's room. Dad's low voice read to his sister. *When out on the lawn there arose such a clatter.* The same words he heard every year on Christmas Eve. At least he didn't have to sit through the story tonight.

The storm had tapered, and moonlight cut through the clouds, lighting up the long icicles that clung to the roof outside of Charlie's bedroom window. Charlie continued to stare at the ceiling, the clock on the desk slowly clicking.

Tick. Tick. Tick.

He just needed to fall asleep, then it would be morning, but his eyes stayed wide open, his mind doing jumping jacks. An uneasy feeling settled in his chest. He glanced out his window. The clouds passed over the moon, darkening the room a shade.

Tick. Tick. Tick.

Why couldn't he fall asleep? He'd never had trouble falling asleep on Christmas Eve before. He rolled over onto his side and fluffed his pillow. Shutting his eyes, the events of the day raced through his mind. He saw himself melting the ornaments. Scribbling over Emily's picture. Biting the head off of her gingerbread man. His mother yelling at him. The wind howling as the tree branches scraped the windowpanes...

Charlie's eyes shot open.

A thump boomed above him, waking him. He'd fallen asleep. Charlie looked at the clock. It was midnight.

Another thump sounded. The house shook and the ceiling rattled. Charlie sat upright. Was the noise coming from... the roof? Charlie listened intently.

Silence.

Maybe he had imagined it. Charlie started to lie back down, when he heard a loud crash.

This time it came from the living room.

3

Up on the rooftop, click click click…

Charlie gripped the edge of his covers, ears straining.

Another patter whumped onto the roof.

Charlie's eyes flew upward, and his heart beat fast in his throat. It was just the snow, he thought. It was just the snow.

Another thump sounded downstairs, and his eyes darted to the door. Was someone in his house?

Charlie jumped out of bed and faced his doorway, his feet frozen to the floor, nothing but the dark hallway before him. He wondered what could've caused the noises.

"Hello?" he called.

Charlie forced himself to exhale. He was being silly. He heard noises in the house all of the time. It was probably just Fluffy. His imagination was getting the best of him.

Or perhaps Emily was playing a prank on him. Maybe she'd finally had enough of his mischief, and she was trying to scare him.

"Hello?" he called again.

He peered deeper into the darkness. Not even the nightlight from the hallway cast its usual gentle glow. Emily must've unplugged it. Charlie's mouth curved up into a slow smile. He could play along.

Charlie slid on his slippers and crept toward the hallway. Moonlight lit his path, and the floor creaked under his feet. Keeping his weight light, he flattened himself against the wall, holding his breath, listening.

Silence.

He tried to think what Emily would do to prank him. Attack him with glitter? Tie him up and paint his nails? Douse him with stinky perfume like those makeup ladies did at the mall? Emily was probably just waiting outside the doorway, ready to leap out and startle him.

Charlie would beat her to it.

Sucking in a breath, he bent his legs and jumped.

"Rawr!" Charlie yelled, springing into the hallway, hands out in front of him like claws.

He paused, waiting for her to scream.

More silence.

Charlie straightened, squinting. Nothing was there but the long stretch of carpet, and the soft sounds of his parents snoring. Emily was more clever than he thought.

If the noises actually came from Emily.

The noises could be something else. Like what? His mind went back to the cat. It wasn't a stretch to think that Fluffy had been plotting her revenge and had decided tonight was the night to attack. Charlie smiled at the thought of Fluffy's retaliation, but then quickly dismissed it.

Charlie made his way down the hall, past the framed baby portraits and the years of school photos—all, in which Charlie had made goofy faces, leaving his parents with no choice but to hang them up anyway. He stopped in front of Emily's bedroom. It had a sparkly, pink "E" hanging on the door, and a sign that read, "Everyone Welcome."

Charlie wrapped his hand around the cool, metal doorknob. The door creaked open, and he peered inside. Lying in the middle of a white, canopy bed, Emily slept, her lacy nightgown identical to the doll next to her. Emily's breaths were slow and steady, her delicate face relaxed into sleep. Fluffy lay curled up at her feet.

Charlie frowned, and clicked the door shut. He scratched his head and glanced around the hall. He started to head back to his room when a scraping noise resonated above him.

Charlie shuffled backward.

More scraping.

Another thunk boomed from the living room, followed by a rustle, and then a clink that sounded like an ornament hitting the floor.

Charlie's pulse rocketed. He opened and closed his hands, tiptoeing to the stairs. He could hear his parents' snoring, and Emily was in her bed. *Who* was in his house? At the top of the staircase, his hand tightened on the banister.

Below him, the embers in the fireplace still burned hot, casting an eerie glow in the living room. He carefully descended, his first step creaking so loud, it could've woken the neighbors.

He paused and listened.

Silence.

Charlie crouched down and peered through the railing. The light from the fireplace cast just enough light to show piles of colorfully wrapped boxes of all shapes and sizes, tied with shimmering, red ribbon, stacked under the Christmas tree.

Charlie's heart leapt.

Presents!

Racing down the stairs, he skipped two steps at a time, not caring if the creaking woke the entire neighborhood. He bounded across the wooden floor and rushed over to the tree. Charlie started sifting through the gifts, searching through the tags, shoving over the ones that didn't say his name. Emily. Mom. Emily. Dad.

Emily.

Emily.

Emily.

Where were his presents?!

Charlie glanced around the living room—at the collection of nativities. The nutcrackers in the corner. The bowl of candy canes on the coffee table. He dug through the presents again thinking that, in his haste, he probably just missed his name. Nothing. His chest tightened and sweat sprung to his forehead.

This didn't make sense. He'd done everything right. He'd been good just long enough so he'd get all the presents he wanted. It had worked every year. Why was this year any different? A sick feeling started to grow in the pit of his stomach. Emily's voice reverberated in his head.

You're going to get a lump of coal in your stocking.

Charlie's head turned to the stockings that hung on the fireplace.

Charlie slowly rose, and stared at the green and red knit stocking, with a beaded white bear on the front. Stitched in a neat scrawl, it read, *Charlie*. The toe of the stocking pointed downward, as if there was something inside, weighing it down.

Placing one foot in front of him, he drew himself forward. The heat from the embers prickled his skin, raising the hairs on the back of his neck. He reached a hand forward and removed the stocking off the mantel. His arm dropped at the weight of the stocking, and his tendons strained.

What was in here?

His heart beat loud in his ears, and his mouth went dry. He tried to swallow, but there was a knot in his throat. Charlie just stood there, staring at the stocking, afraid to reach his hand inside.

I'm being ridiculous, he thought. *Just stick your hand inside.*

He sucked in a sharp breath and reached inside.

His hand connected with something cold, and hard. His fingers curled around the object, some spots slippery and smooth, other spots rough. He tightened his grip, and clenched his eyes shut.

No.

It couldn't be.

But he knew what it was without removing it. Charlie pulled it out, and turned it over in his hand, opening his eyes.

His stomach lurched, and he blinked.

Coal.

This wasn't happening. This wasn't possible. His parents wouldn't be so cruel—or Emily, where would she have found a lump of coal? Charlie glanced down at the dish of cookies Emily had left for Santa. It was empty save for a few crumbs, and a small smear of green frosting. The glass of milk was half gone. A note card next to it read, "*For Santa.*"

Santa.

The word floated in Charlie's head. Santa. But he didn't believe in Santa, so how could *he* give him coal? There was no way he could have been wrong about Santa being real. Could he? Not after all these years.

This had to be a joke. All the clues had "prank" written all over them: The sounds on the roof. The lack of presents. The cookie crumbs and half-drunken milk. They all had to be related. Yes, someone was playing a trick on him.

But Charlie stood frozen, staring at the rock in his hand. It felt like a hundred pounds—and it grew heavier by the second. The glowing embers in the fireplace reflected off the ornaments, looking like fifty sets of evil eyes, staring back at him, mocking him.

"Looks like someone's out of bed," a scratchy voice said from behind.

"Aye," another voice answered. "That ruins all the fun. I was hoping to wake him by nibbling on his toes."

Charlie tightened his shoulders.

He slowly turned around.

A tiny bell jingled.

4.

Deck the halls...

Two silhouetted figures lingered in the entryway. Smaller than children, their dark forms stood chest high to Charlie, their figures gaunt and bony. One leaned against the wall, arms crossed, and the other picked at his teeth. The dying light from the fireplace washed over their faces, highlighting leathered skin and saggy wrinkles.

Those weren't children.

Charlie rubbed his eyes, blinking.

They were still there.

Charlie moved his mouth open and closed, but nothing came out.

"What's the matter?" one of them asked. "Never seen an elf before?"

Charlie's eyebrows squished together. "A w-what?"

The other elf let out a loud cackle. He slapped a hand on his knee. "Children these days. They really are dim."

Charlie swallowed and scrubbed his palms on his thighs. "Who are you? Who are you, really?"

The elf smiled, and pointy teeth—teeth that looked like the tips of sucked candy canes—flashed in the dim light. "Oh, he's one of *those* kids. An unbeliever. This should be fun. Can I have first crack at him?"

Charlie took a step back. He had to be dreaming. This wasn't real. Any minute now and he'd wake up. That would explain everything.

"I don't know," the other elf said, voice raspy. "I saw him first. And it has been too long since..." The elf peered down at Charlie's feet. "...I've snacked on some toes."

"My toes?"

"Sure. If Jack Frost can nip at your nose, then I should be allowed to nibble on your toes." The elves laughed in unison.

Like puppets on a string, the elves straightened, stepping forward at the same time, and stalked toward him. The elves slunk deeper into the living room, the light illuminating them further.

Lines creased every inch of their faces, their skin a yellowish hue. Slanted eyes and sharp ears, their chins jutted out in front of them, with prickly hairs on the end. Ragged breeches and tattered sackcloth shirts covered their frail bodies, veins showing through their thinly muscled arms and gnarled fingers. Rusted jingle bells dangled on the end of their frayed shoes, a few crusted toenails peeking through. One elf's nose was slightly more crooked, the other had bushier eyebrows.

Charlie shook his head back and forth. "This isn't real," he told himself. "This isn't real."

"You better watch out. You better not cry," the elf with the bushy eyebrows said. "That song exists for a reason. It's always worse for those who struggle."

Charlie staggered backwards, tripping over the rug.

The elves glided in closer, their gate slow and smooth, the rusty bells on their shoes jingling a sour note with every step. They narrowed their eyes, red beginning to glow around the irises, spreading out to their eyelids. Charlie's gaze shot to Emily's crumpled picture by the fire—to the elves he'd drawn with the glowing, red eyes.

Not possible.

The elves' mouths stretched into wicked smiles, the light from the fireplace highlighting their yellow rancid teeth.

"It's just a dream," Charlie said, backing away. "Wake up." He slapped his cheeks. He shouldn't have eaten that gingerbread.

The elves sidled closer, their ruby eyes now brighter than the bulbs on the tree.

"Stay back," Charlie warned, but his heart was drumming wildly.

"Or what?" Their tongues darted out, their smiles widening.

Thinking fast, Charlie pointed past the elves. "Look! Santa!"

The elves turned.

Charlie took off. He dashed toward the stairs, his pulse racing, his feet pounding.

Two new elves sprung from the front foyer, blocking the stairway. Their hands reached toward him, their yellow fingernails long and jagged, their eyes also illuminating red.

Charlie pitched sideways, bumping into the grandfather clock in the front foyer, his mind doing cartwheels. Charlie sprinted down the dark hallway. Two more elves emerged from the kitchen. Charlie skidded to a stop.

The elves advanced, nothing but two burning eyes approaching from the front, and two floating eyes drawing close from behind. His head darted side to side, his breaths pumping fast. Charlie ran into the dining room and slid across the hardwood floors, and underneath the dining table, disappearing behind his mother's good holiday tablecloth, its fringe almost touching the floor, obscuring Charlie from view.

Charlie held his breath, his pulse thumping in his ears, daring not to make a sound. He didn't know why his family hadn't heard the commotion. They should be rushing downstairs. Maybe the elves had gotten to them and hurt them. No, this was a dream, he reminded himself. But what if it wasn't? He needed to get upstairs and see if they were okay.

A floorboard creaked, and Charlie stiffened.

Through the fringe of the tablecloth, Charlie watched as six pairs of elven feet crept into the room. He froze as their feet passed him, the corroded bells on their shoes softly jingling. They spilt on either side of him, circling the table. Charlie pulled in a breath, keeping himself as quiet as possible. Their breaths rasped on the air, each inhale and exhale resonating through the room.

Charlie listened intently for the bells to pass, giving him the opening he needed to make a run for the stairs. He readied himself, counting to three in his mind. *One. Two. Three...*

Charlie paused.

Wait.

It was too silent.

Where were the jingle bells?

The floor creaked behind him, and Charlie flung around.

The elf with the crooked nose appeared, his head popping underneath the table. He leaned inward and smiled, his breath stinking like rotten eggs. His long, gnarly fingers reached for Charlie's slippers, and Charlie scrambled backward, kicking his legs out in front of him.

The elf continued forward, undeterred. "How's about a little snack?" he said, snatching Charlie's foot. He started to tug off one slipper, his sharp nail scraping Charlie's heel.

Charlie couldn't go down like this. Dream or not, this elf's face couldn't be the last thing he saw. Charlie narrowed his eyes, and he set his jaw. He drew back his foot, and using all the strength he had, he kicked the elf in the face.

The elf howled and grabbed his crooked nose, flying backwards, knocking the rest of the elves over like bowling pins.

Seizing the moment, Charlie leapt out from under the table, and tore across the stretch of the dark dining room and made it to the stairs. His feet tripped as he stumbled in his slippers, and they flew off in different directions. Footsteps pounded after him. The stairs squeaked as he rushed upward, and Charlie *wished* they would wake the whole neighborhood.

Charlie made it to the landing and bolted down the hallway

toward his bedroom. Once inside, he slammed his door shut, raced over to his desk and rummaged through the piles of junk.

Come on, come on, where are they?

For the first time in his life, Charlie cursed at his inability to keep a clean room.

Aha!

Charlie snatched a small, velvet bag from his junk drawer, and dumped out an entire bag of marbles onto the floor. He could hear the elves pattering up the hallway. He put his hand on his doorknob, and timing it just right, swung open his door. All six of the elves rushed inside.

The elves hit the marbles, slipping and sliding across the floor, arms flailing and legs kicking, their wrinkled faces open in confusion. The bells on their toes all jingled in a deranged tune. They rammed into the wall across the room with a *jingled-thud.*

Charlie ran from his room, pulling the door closed behind him. He stared at the doorknob. Because of his mother's love of design, every antique doorknob in the Peters' household had a skeleton key placed in the keyhole. If ever his mother's love for the details ever came in handy, it was now. He grabbed the key and turned. Pounding and scratching came from the other side of the door. *It had worked!* The elves were locked inside.

"Mom! Dad!" he yelled, reaching his parent's door. He twisted the doorknob, but it wouldn't turn. He rattled the handle again, searched for their antique key, but it was mysteriously gone.

What?

He banged on the door.

"Mom! Dad! Wake up!"

He could hear his parents' snoring. Why couldn't they hear him? Why weren't they waking up?

"Emily!" Charlie ran to her room and launched his shoulder into the wood. The sparkly "E" on her door fell to the floor as the door crashed open.

"Emily!" Charlie said with relief, seeing his sister on the bed, curled up with her doll snuggled in her arms.

Charlie sprinted over and shook her shoulders. "Emily, wake up."

Her eyelids fluttered open, but her eyes just stared straight in front of her, unmoving at the ceiling.

"Emily? Are you okay?"

Charlie shook her again, his fingers digging into her nightgown, but her face was motionless, calm. Her gaze seemed far away, as if living in another time—her breaths still slow and even.

"Emily, come on! Wake up!"

Charlie waved his hands in front of her face. That's when he noticed that Fluffy, who would have hissed and fled the room at Charlie's mere presence, remained asleep at Emily's feet.

This didn't make sense. Charlie didn't know what was wrong with her or Fluffy. He didn't know why his parent's door was locked. Why there was an army of elves after him. And why he couldn't wake up from this dream that didn't feel like a dream.

"Emily, *please!*"

Charlie's shoulder's sagged.

A sharp nail tapped him on the back, and Charlie slowly turned. His eyes widened at two silhouettes before him—two elves hovering over him at the foot of the bed.

In his peripheral vision, he noticed a few more shadows approach. Charlie realized that there were *eight* elves instead of six. A scream trapped in his throat as they threw a burlap sack over his head and body. The sack cinched in tight, and darkness closed in.

34

5.

Chestnuts roasting on an open fire...

Tiny feet scurried, and miniature hands held Charlie aloft.

Through the sack, Charlie's breaths were low and shallow, and snorts and chortles resounded around him. Charlie's head bounced and his teeth jarred together, as the elves scuttled down the stairs.

"Mom! Dad!" he choked out, but his voice was muffled.

The elves whipped him around a corner, and Charlie's body flopped like a rag doll, before a whoosh of heat hit his face. Sharp nails poked through the sack as Charlie's body was flipped upright. The heat travelled along his arms and torso, down his legs and feet. Charlie writhed and squirmed. He pushed his hands outward, and his palms connected with hard stone on either side of him.

"Up, we go!" a gruff voice said.

Sweat slid down the sides of Charlie's neck, sticking his pajamas to his back.

Was he in... *the chimney*?

Charlie squinted through the dark, but he couldn't see a thing. Tiny hands pushed and shoved, forcing his body up the tight space. Charlie could feel the hard walls of the chimney tight on all sides of his body. He wished he knew where they were taking him.

Inch by inch, he was thrust upward, and Charlie tried to wriggle free in the suffocating area, not sure whether he wanted to continue up or retreat back down. He squeezed his eyes shut, wishing he were anywhere but here—anywhere but trapped in this flue with these determined little creatures.

The heat faded the further he rose. His elbows were crushed into his sides, but he was able to poke a finger through the front of the sack near his face, widening a hole in its loose weave, just enough to see. Brisk, night air seeped in, filling Charlie's lungs, and he gasped. Through the small opening, stars speckled the midnight sky, and Charlie's eyebrows shot up. He was on the roof.

"One! Two! Three!" the elves said together.

Charlie was hoisted upward.

"Let me go!" Charlie shouted.

He punched and kicked, beating his arms and legs inside the sack, ordering them to release him. The elves laughed and tossed him forward. Charlie fell, landing hard on his backside. He lay stunned on a hard surface, his breath hot against the cloth sack. Through the hole, he could see that he was on a seat—in some sort of open vehicle.

Like a sleigh?

He shook his head. He couldn't believe he'd just thought that. As if there were a sleigh on top of his roof. The back of Charlie's throat ached. His mind had started to believe this nightmare. He needed to get out of here and back into his bed, where he could wake up and have a normal Christmas morning.

The elves bustled about, puttering around him. A slam echoed, followed by dozens of dissonant jingles. A few of the elves snickered off to the side. Maybe he could untie the sack while they were distracted. Maybe he could sneak away without them realizing. Charlie reached down to his feet, zeroing in on the sack opening. He fumbled with the rope threaded through the rough material, trying to loosen the knot that kept the cinch shut.

"Ready?" an elf called.

"Ready!" the rest yelled together.

Charlie's heart accelerated.

His fingers throbbed, and his knuckles burned red, but he

frantically picked at the knot. One loop pulled free.

Yes!

Charlie grunted, and his pulse skipped. He dug his fingers in deeper and loosened another loop. Two more knots, and then he'd be free.

"The North Pole!" one of the elves called out.

The vehicle lurched, and Charlie's fingers slipped. He flew backwards with a thunk, his shoulder ramming into the hard backseat. The vehicle whizzed forward in a swoosh, and Charlie felt his stomach drop. He worked his finger through the hole he'd made earlier, tugging it open even wider, and peered out.

His mouth flopped open.

The sky raced above him, the stars zooming past him like firecrackers. Cold air bit his cheeks, and the whistling wind stung his eyes.

No.

This wasn't real. This wasn't possible.

If this *was* a sleigh, and if this *was* some sort of Christmas nightmare, there weren't any reindeer in front. Whatever was powering this thing, it was flying on its own. He strained his eyes as far as they would reach. Two elves sat next to him, and the rest sat in front. He could barely see over the tops of their grimy heads. The elves grinned as they flew, their teeth sharp and bright as the moon shone down.

Charlie focused back on the knots.

He reached down and tugged at the rope. The ties unfastened. Charlie's pace quickened. He was almost free. Yes, he wouldn't be able to escape now—not with flying thousands of feet in the air—but wherever they were taking him, whenever they landed, he'd be able to run.

Without warning, the sack opened wide, and the elf Charlie had kicked in the nose earlier poked his head inside.

"Ah-ah-ahhhh. No peeking for naughty boys." His red eyes flashed.

Charlie flinched, and his heart took off.

Drooping skin folded back as the elf's mouth spread into a sinister smile. His putrid, foul breath filled the sack.

"If this is Santa's sleigh where are all the reindeer?' Charlie demanded.

"Ha!" the elf replied. "Those reindeer are all for show. It completes Santa's look."

Another elf smacked him upside the head.

"Ow! What was that for?" the crooked-nose elf said, rubbing his ear.

"Don't be giving away Santa's secrets, you dolt!"

The elf's face paled, before he turned back to Charlie.

"Bye, bye." His mangled hand reached downward.

"No!" Charlie yelled. "Wait! Don't!"

His fingernails closed in, and the elf pulled the cinch tight.

Charlie pounded his fists into the heavy sack. "Take me home!"

Charlie continued to yell, but the elves ignored him. He pleaded, until his throat burned. Charlie finally collapsed, pressing his palms into his eyes.

The longer they flew, the more somber the elves became. No more laughter, no more threats of eating toes, no more red eyes or sharp nails. Just silence as they traveled through the night air.

Charlie's teeth began to chatter, and he wrapped his arms around himself. Chills spread over his body, and he shivered. Time passed. He didn't know how long he sat there, shaking. It could've been hours or minutes. He tucked his knees up to his chest, his gaze locked on the coarse, brown bag. Just when he was convinced he'd never be warm again, a wave of hot, stale air settled over him.

The flying vehicle pitched and swerved. Charlie's head slammed back as the vehicle connected with hard earth. The vehicle jolted to a stop, and Charlie gripped onto his knees tight.

The bells on the elves' shoes jingled and then faded into the distance.

Silence fell.

Charlie sat, trembling, nothing heard but his breathing loud in his ears. He waited. Was that it? Were the elves just going to abandon him, alone, in this sack to die?

He pulled in another breath. The air stuck to his skin, sweat gathering on his temples.

A dingy bell jingled. A pair of arms snatched him up from behind, flipped him up, and dumped him out of the sack and onto the rocky ground like he was a giant potato. Charlie groaned, and peeled his face off of the stone floor.

"What's going on? Where are we?" Charlie asked.

The elf only smiled.

Charlie's brow furrowed. He watched the elf scurry out of sight, down a long tunnel.

He took in his surroundings. Spiky walls towered above him, with jagged, rock walls on either side of him. Trails of water leaked from the ceiling, the musty scent filling Charlie's nose. Torches stretched from one end of the area to the other, the warm glow highlighting the dank space.

They were in a cave.

Charlie jumped to his feet and scrubbed the dirt off his hands. He rushed over to the cave opening, and set his hands on the cool, bumpy walls, peeking over the edge. Charlie scuffled back, eyes bulging. The cave dropped off a hundred feet below, nothing but a black abyss beneath him, a swirl of white fog snaking around the darkness.

No.

He couldn't be trapped here. Why had the elves brought him here? There had to be a way out—a way back home.

The vehicle.

Charlie's gaze slid to the left.

He froze.

Rusted and red, the massive vehicle sat in the torchlight, the streams of yellow light dancing across the decrepit, old structure. Where paint didn't flake, the rest was corroded, metal spots tarnished with a green hue. It looked like something out of a storybook—a haunted version of *'Twas a Night Before Christmas*. There were no reigns. No reindeer. No Santa. No gifts.

But.

It was *a sleigh.*

Charlie's legs ached and his eyes burned. He stood staring at the red sleigh, his bare feet glued to the dusty ground. The dripping water from the cave walls reverberated in the silence. The torches lining the cave flickered.

Heavy footsteps sounded down the tunnel.

Charlie's head snapped up, and he swallowed the knot in his throat. He squinted, as a shadow lengthened on the tunnel wall in front of him. Whatever it was, it was getting closer.

6.

Now, Dasher. Now, Dancer. Now, Prancer and Vixen...

"Hello?" Charlie asked. "Who's there?"

Footsteps approached, clopping like a horse. Charlie's mind raced, and he glanced around the cave once more, but there was no escape. The sound of keys clanging together echoed through the cavern.

Clop. Clink. Clop. Clink.

Charlie edged backward.

Clop. Clink. Clop. Clink.

A massive silhouette filled the tunnel opening, the creature's shoulders almost reaching the width of the walls, his height the length of the entryway.

Charlie scrambled back, pressing himself against the side of the decrepit, old sleigh.

The thing stepped into the light, giving Charlie his first glimpse of the creature. It stood seven feet tall, with the body of a reindeer, and the torso of a man, with a rack of antlers spouting from its beastly head.

Muscles bulged from its bare chest and arms, shags of fur hanging around its reindeer ears and snout. A coiled whip hung from its belt, along with a heavy set of keys and a leather pouch. Black eyes focused in on Charlie's thin form, a smile curling along its lips.

Charlie tensed, and glanced around at the cave walls. No exit, save for the cliff that dropped a hundred feet down.

It was just a dream, Charlie thought again. Just another part of this long, weird dream. But it wasn't. Charlie was beginning to think this was real. Deep in his gut, he knew this was real.

Charlie tightened his fists.

"Who are you?" Charlie asked. "Why did you and your freaky little elves bring me here?" Inside, he was trembling, but he wouldn't show that to this beast. He was sick of feeling afraid.

Silence echoed in the large cavern. The torches casted eerie shadows on the creature's hairy face.

Finally, the thing's mouth twitched, and he rolled his beefy shoulders. "I am Blitzen. I am your warden, your enemy and your darkest nightmare. You've been sentenced to work here in the coal mines." He smiled, and his large, square teeth were yellow in the dim light.

"What?" Charlie asked. "Coal mines? What do you mean coal mines?"

A faint memory came to mind, and he shivered.

It's not like Santa has a coal mine at the North Pole.

Charlie stared at the beast, and more memories tickled the back of his mind. The crayons. Emily shoving the picture in his face. The reindeer he'd distorted.

The Minotaur.

Blitzen looked *exactly* like the Minotaur he'd drawn in Emily's picture.

"No," Charlie said, shaking his head. "There's a mistake. I shouldn't be here—"

"We never make mistakes." The beast snorted, flaring his nostrils.

Charlie put his fingers to his temples and kneaded in circles.

Blitzen hefted a massive, leather book in his arms. A swirl of intricate symbols and pictures were engraved onto the worn casing. Charlie peered closer. Doves. Horns. A sleigh. Stockings.

Blitzen flipped open the book and lifted up a feather pen.

"Tell me your name."

Charlie's forehead creased. "What?"

"Your name," Blitzen barked. "*What is it?*"

"C—"

Charlie paused.

Blitzen raised his thick brows.

Blitzen didn't know his name. Which meant he didn't know who he was. Maybe it *was* a mistake Charlie was here. Or if it wasn't a mistake, maybe Charlie had a chance to escape before they discovered his real identity. He could get back home to his warm bed. Back home to his presents and away from this nightmare.

"My name is Ch—Chester... Mc—McScrooge." Charlie twisted his face. It was a horrible cover, but it was the first thing he could think of. He'd been forced to watch *A Christmas Carol* the day before, and the name "Scrooge" was stuck in his head. Blitzen would for sure know it was a lie. Charlie held his breath and clenched his eyes shut. He peeked one eye open, waiting for the consequences.

"Mc... *Scrooge?*" Blitzen pressed his hairy lips together.

"Er... Yup."

Blitzen scribbled the name down. "Well. You, Chester McScrooge are now on the Naughty List. You will work in the coal

48

mines until you have earned your way onto the Nice List. *If* you earn your way back onto the Nice List." He lifted a brow. "However—" Blitzen shuffled forward and loomed over Charlie. His gaze darkened and a vein pulsed in his neck. "I'll be watching you. There are those who have been… *unsatisfied* with their new life here and have tried to leave prematurely." He narrowed his eyes. "Trust me, bad things happen to those who don't follow the rules of the mines."

Blitzen slammed the book shut.

Charlie flinched.

"March."

"*March*?"

"March!" Blitzen shoved Charlie forward.

Rocks bit into the bottom of Charlie's bare feet and his breath fogged out in front of him.

Charlie lifted his legs and marched.

Blitzen's footsteps echoed off the cave walls as they headed deeper into the cave. Each step grated along Charlie's bones. Light from the torches danced on the tunnel walls, morphing and changing, messing with Charlie's vision.

Thoughts bounced inside of Charlie's head. He could try to take

49

off now. Try and outrun Blitzen and make it back to the sleigh—try and start the sleigh. But what if he couldn't? He looked around the cave. Who knew when or if the elves would appear. They were probably hiding. And then there was Blitzen's warning of bad things happening to those who didn't follow the rules of the mines. Who knew what *that* meant. No, he needed to wait it out. Gather information. He might only have one chance at escape.

Blitzen shoved him again.

"I'm moving!" Charlie glared back at the beast.

Up ahead, a rusted elevator sat at the end of the cave, covered by an eroded, scissored gate. Blitzen clopped over, his hooves thumping on the stone floor. He opened the gate, and motioned Charlie inside.

"In," Blitzen said.

Charlie stepped back and stuffed his hands into his armpits.

Blitzen growled. "In."

Charlie stood frozen, staring at the corroded, metal contraption. The elevator groaned, creaking as it swayed. Charlie's stomach flipped. He had a feeling if he went down, he would never return.

Charlie backed up another step. "Uh uh. No way. No way I'm getting in there."

Blitzen ground his teeth. He was next to Charlie in two steps. He grasped him by the ear and dragged him over.

"*In*, I said." He pushed him inside.

"Ow!" Charlie clutched the side of his head.

The elevator lurched under Charlie's feet. He threw out his arms and fell back against the cool, metal box, steadying himself. The elevator swayed again as Blitzen's hefty form squeezed inside. He closed the gate, the metal screeching, resounding inside the shaft.

Blitzen pulled down a heavy lever, and the gears kick-started, slowly churning.

The elevator jolted and began to descend.

Charlie's lungs tightened. He couldn't breathe. He should've run when he had the chance.

Blitzen turned to Charlie, his eyes sparkling, his lips twisting up into a snarl. "Take one last look. It might be your last."

Charlie's eyes darted between the beast and the disappearing cavern above him. He held his breath, gulping, taking one last glimpse of the world, before all he saw was black.

7.

And two eyes made out of coal…

Down.

Down.

Down.

Stale, dark air whizzed past Charlie's face as the elevator plummeted into a black ravine. Charlie's stomach flew up into his throat, and he gripped onto the elevator gate tight, clamping down hard on his teeth. Blitzen stood next to him, arms crossed, his body a brick in the storm.

The elevator screeched to a stop.

Blitzen reached forward and slammed open the scissored gate. Its rusted hinges screaked, echoing in the darkness before him.

"Out."

Charlie edged out of the metal box. Anywhere was better than being in there—but the air was even more stagnant down here.

As Blitzen squeezed out of the elevator, the beast's eyes

hollowed in the dim light, highlighted from another torch connected to a rocky wall on his left.

Damp dirt squished between Charlie's toes, and pebbles jabbed underneath his feet. He peered out in front of him as far as he could see. Tiny specks of bright lights floated to and fro, flickering in and out of his vision. Low bangs and high-pitched clangs reverberated from the dark space. Charlie blinked, and his eyes adjusted a tad.

Rocky walls jutted inward, creating a long, narrow tunnel, the ceiling hanging low. Charlie squinted, not able to see how deep the shaft extended.

Charlie's eyes adjusted further. He started noticing details like a rail track coming from the depths of the mine shaft. The track curved left where it terminated at a massive conveyor belt, squeaking as it moved and churned, stretching flat, until it led upwards at a sharp angle. Charlie bent down, trying to see where it went, but it disappeared behind a large outcropping.

Charlie swept his gaze to the right, taking in a thick, wooden door with large iron hinges and a matching doorknob. He searched for another sign of exit. Nothing. He scrubbed the end of his nose.

"Come on," Blitzen said, shoving Charlie forward.

Charlie stumbled, catching his toe on the hard steel rail track. He hissed and hopped on one foot.

"Where are you taking me?" Charlie demanded.

Blitzen didn't respond. He just headed into the tunnel, toward the floating lights. Charlie gritted his teeth and followed.

Large timber beams about every twenty feet or so lined the walls from floor to ceiling with an equally large beam resting atop, acting as support to keep the tunnel from collapsing. Water dripped from above, and Charlie dodged the drops, trying not to get wet. His foot splashed into a puddle, soaking the bottoms of his red and black pajamas. He wished he'd had his slippers.

Charlie noticed that the rail branched off down adjacent tunnels. He could see fainter lights and hear the sounds of metal striking rock down each one, but he and Blitzen continued on the main track. To Charlie's left, he noticed a tunnel running parallel to the one he currently traveled down. Its access was blocked by signs that read *DANGER* and *KEEP OUT*. Up ahead, silhouetted figures came into focus, bodies shifting, arms moving up and down. The clanging intensified. A flash of light seared along a silver blade.

For the first time, the mine scene came to life.

Another Minotaur-like reindeer held a whip with the name, *"Dancer"* etched onto the handle. The beast paced, patrolling a group of kids who tirelessly banged their axes into the hard rock wall. A group of children fiddled with the lamps on their helmets (*that's where the lights were coming from!*), while another reindeer beast—with the name of *"Dasher"* carved onto his leather vest—yelled at them to hurry up.

Charlie noticed small birdcages interspaced throughout the mine, each one containing a dove.

"Hey! Get off the track!" a young voice yelled from behind.

Charlie leapt, turning, just in time to see two kids struggling to push a loaded mine cart past him. Sweat shone on their faces, their tendons straining in their arms. The cart was filled with small black rocks, and Charlie's jaw dropped.

Coal.

His heart skipped a beat.

This really was a coal mine. And the miners were kids. All of them.

How long had they been trapped down here? Did their parents know? Why hadn't anyone done anything about this? This wasn't right.

Charlie watched as the children continued to push the cart up the mine shaft. They disappeared, but he could hear the coal being dumped onto what he assumed was the conveyer belt.

As Charlie passed, children turned and looked over their shoulders, eyes wide, mouths open, but they quickly returned to work, as their reindeer guardians cracked their whips.

Off-key bells jingled to his left, and an elf covered in soot, scuttled up from the darkness. Charlie eyed the rusted bells on the elf's tattered shoes.

"Helmet and pick axe," the elf said. "As you ordered, Blitzen, sir."

Blitzen snatched the objects and thrust them into Charlie's arms. Charlie grunted at the impact, staggering. Charlie glanced down at the items.

"No," he said to Blitzen. "I'm not doing this. I'm not working in this mine. You can't make me. Take me home!"

Blitzen turned on him so fast he didn't have time to blink.

Air whooshed into Charlie's face as Blitzen's hand grabbed the collar of his pajama shirt. He flattened Charlie against the spiky wall. Charlie's feet dangled off the ground.

"I told you bad things happened to those who didn't follow the rules of the mine," Blitzen growled. "Do you or do you *not* want to find out what that means?"

Charlie struggled to free himself from Blitzen's grasp, trying to pry the large fingers off of him.

Blitzen lifted a thick brow.

Charlie held his breath, but he finally nodded his head.

Blitzen released his grip and Charlie dropped to the ground, exhaling.

"Pick yourself up," Blitzen barked.

Charlie struggled to stand. He rubbed his neck, trembling, but gathered his strength and followed Blitzen across the rails.

Blitzen led Charlie over to a small alcove on the edge of the mine.

Three children worked alone, lifting their axes, and pounding the sharp blades into the black, solid rock. Sweat ran down their faces, mingling with dirt on their skin, leaving streaks.

The tallest of the three caught his eyes first. She turned, locking her gaze with his. Wearing a white tank top and plaid pajama bottoms, her long, sinewy arms were surprisingly strong. Her auburn hair was pulled back into a high ponytail, with a few loose strands curling around her sweaty forehead, and a beauty mark, just by her right eye.

A small, scrawny boy—about half the size of Charlie—had a mop of sandy hair that hung in shags over his face. He hid behind the girl, halfway in the shadows, wearing footed, one-piece pajamas with pictures of Santa all over them. As Charlie drew near, the boy gasped, revealing a large gap between his two front teeth.

The third kid, a beefy, freckled boy a couple of years older than Charlie, wore ripped jeans and a t-shirt, as if that was what he'd worn to bed. With brush-cut hair, and smirk that would make Charlie jealous, he turned and lifted his brows as the two approached.

"This is your team," Blitzen said. "That's all you need to know about them. Now figure out the rules or you'll end up like Timmy."

Blitzen pulled out the hefty, leather book Charlie had seen on the surface. The lamps from his three teammates' helmets highlighted the now familiar symbols on the binding. Blitzen turned, and clomped over to the center of the mine.

"What's he doing?" Charlie asked. "And who's Timmy?"

The beefy kid pushed off the wall, and his freckles and round face came to light as he barged in close. "Oooo. My favorite part. Things are about to get exciting."

The girl rolled her eyes. "You're sick."

She leaned in to Charlie and nodded toward Blitzen. "I don't know who Timmy is, but we're about to find out. That's the Naughty and Nice List."

Blitzen turned the pages, the sound of crackling paper bouncing off the cave walls. Blitzen lifted the book upwards, until it settled in the crook of his muscled arm.

"Timmy Fairchild!" His voice boomed through the cavern. All activity stopped and the miners turned.

A young boy around Charlie's age sprung from a group of boys on the left. He gave a yelp and rushed forward.

"Finally!" he said. "Finally, I've made it onto the Nice List!"

Blitzen's eyes darkened, narrowing to pin points. "You, Timmy Fairchild, are hereby sentenced to the Permanent Naughty List."

Timmy faltered. His eyes widened and his face paled.

"No," he whispered. "No."

Timmy scrambled away, his head darting side to side. Sweat beaded on his forehead.

"I won't go!" Timmy continued to edge backward, and the boys and girls moved aside, parting a path for him.

Blitzen slowly stalked forward.

Timmy elbowed kids away from him, shoving his way through the crowd, away from Blitzen and the book.

Dasher pulled out his whip.

Dancer cracked his knuckles.

Timmy bolted.

"Stop him!" Blitzen shouted.

Reindeers charged inward. Timmy ducked through the crowd of kids. Chaos erupted.

Charlie watched the scene before him with his mouth parted—at the mass of glowing lamps and swirling black figures.

"He doesn't have a chance," the girl whispered in Charlie's ear. She chewed the end of her thumbnail. "I'll bet you five bucks that he's found in thirty seconds flat."

"Why run?" Charlie asked. "I mean... where's he gonna go?"

The girl smoothed down the bottom of her long ponytail. "Everyone tries to run at some point. It doesn't matter if you have a place to go or not. The mine breaks you one way or another."

"I'm Rose, by the way." She wiped off her palm and reached out a hand. "And that's Henry," she said, pointing at the scrawny boy. The boy's eyes widened and he scuttered backward, flattening himself up against the cave wall. "He doesn't speak," Rose said. "Never has. Don't ask me how I know his name."

Charlie took her hand and shook it, her long fingers crushing his. Charlie winced, and pulled back his hand.

"And that's Zach." She pointed over to the larger boy with freckles.

"And you are?" Rose asked.

"Oh, Ch—" Charlie paused. He'd told Blitzen a different name up on the surface. He'd better be consistent. "Er... Chester."

"Chester," Rose said. "Alright. Chester it is."

Zach snorted from the corner. "Nice name, Chesterrrr."

Charlie wanted to respond, but Timmy's wide eyes and frazzled hair popped up in front of his face.

"Help me!" he said.

Charlie jerked backward, and words choked in his throat.

Timmy took off again, but Zach stuck out his foot.

Timmy tripped, and fell on his face, his cheek scraping hard against a rock. Zach barked out a laugh.

Silence fell.

The children parted and the reindeers put away their whips. Timmy spit out a mouthful of dirt and raised his head, a large red gash streaked his cheek.

Two elves scurried forward as Blitzen clopped over to the boy, hovering above him.

"Timmy was found lingering out of line yesterday," Blitzen said, voice booming. "Wandering too far off from his team. A lesson for you all."

"N-No!" Timmy said. "No! I won't do it again! I promise! Please. Please!"

The elves smiled, their jagged teeth as sharp as the silver blades around them. They hoisted Timmy up by the arms, and dragged him backwards, Timmy's heels digging into the mud as he slid away.

The kids stood silent as they watched Timmy's small form stuffed into the elevator at the far end of the mine. Instead of going back up to the surface where Charlie had entered, the elevator descended further into the mountain, deeper down the shaft.

Charlie stood transfixed, his eyes glued to the scene.

"Back to work!!" Blitzen's voice echoed off the walls. The children slowly turned back to their work.

"What... what just happened?" Charlie asked. "What's the... *Permanent Naughty List?*"

Rose opened her mouth to answer, but Zach nudged her out of the way, planting his feet out to the side, his smirk up to his ears.

"It means you *never* leave," Zach said. "Once you go down, you don't ever come back up."

Charlie swallowed hard. If this *was* a dream, he wanted to wake up... now.

8.

Guide us to thy perfect light…

Charlie fiddled with his lamp.

An old miner's helmet, it wasn't the usual headlamp. Not an easy flashlight with a switch that simply turned the light on and off, this was a corroded cylinder canister that was clipped onto the front of the helmet—with a spout for a flame that burned outward from the center of the reflector disk.

On the top, a dial could twist back and forth to release water into the cylinder to the bottom of the device where a couple of calcium carbide rocks sat, causing the chemical reaction necessary to ignite a flame. The contraption wasn't anything Charlie had ever seen. It was like something from his great-great-grandfather's time.

Charlie struck the flint and a small flame emerged, but it wasn't bright enough. It was a dull, pathetic flicker. Charlie squinted through the dark. His teammates had gone back to work, their backs to him, their axes swinging up and down.

"Hey, guys," Charlie said. "Could you... show me how this thing works?"

He waved his hand in front of the pitiful flame, and the heat warmed his skin. He shook the helmet, then banged on the top of it. "I can barely see."

Rose, Henry, and Zach ignored him. They just lifted their axes up and pummeled them down onto the hard, rock wall. Charlie peeked behind him. Blitzen could appear any second. Who knew what Blitzen would do if he saw that he wasn't working. Not that he was afraid of him, Charlie reminded himself. Just that he needed to play it cool. He needed to figure things out, stay out of trouble, until he could think of his next move. Timmy might have not made it out, but that wasn't going to be Charlie's fate.

The flame on his helmet dimmed another degree.

"Guys! A little help?"

Henry turned, and Charlie pointed to his lamp.

Henry's lips quivered, and he turned back to the wall. Above him, the dove in the cage flapped its wings. At least the bird seemed to care. Charlie wondered again why they kept doves down here.

Charlie heaved out a breath.

"Fine," he mumbled to himself.

Charlie wrapped his fingers around the dial at the top of the rusted cylinder. He had no idea what he was doing, but it couldn't be that hard. He'd watched the other kids turn the dials—perhaps that was the answer. His fingertips gripped the tarnished metal, the grooves digging into his skin, and turned.

A huge flash of white light blinded his eyes.

Charlie flew backward, dust and bits of rock fell from the low ceiling into the puddle of water that had gathered on the ground below. Ringing sounded in Charlie's ears.

"What the heck is your problem!" Rose yanked Charlie upward. "You can't add that much water!"

Snickers erupted from the next group over. The children covered their mouths and fingers pointed in Charlie's direction.

Rose's fingernails bit into Charlie's arm as she pulled him to the side. "Do you *want* to get us all in trouble? You can only turn the dial a notch. A few drops are plenty to create a strong enough flame. Besides, we only get so much water and calcium carbide to last us each the day."

Zach set his axe down and leaned an elbow onto the handle. "I don't know why you're helping him. I say you let him dig his own grave.

I mean, look at him. He's got Permanent Naughty List written all over him. Anyone with a name like *Chester* would."

Rose threw Zach a glare.

"What'd you do to land yourself in here, anyway?" Zach asked Charlie. "Pranks on your teachers at school? Not listening to your parents? Did you not believe in Santa?" He gave him a knowing look. "Though, I bet it's nothing worse than Henry over there. I don't know what he's done, but that little dude's got secrets."

Henry's eyes grew wide and he pressed deeper into the shadows.

Zach cupped a hand to his mouth. "Of course, I'm not afraid of him. I'm not afraid of anybody!" His voiced echoed down the shaft.

"Shh! Keep your voice down!" Rose hissed. "We haven't fixed Chester's lamp yet!"

Zach smiled. "Exactly."

Footsteps clopped, and a whip cracked. Rose's face went white.

"Sorry, Ches," she whispered. "You're on your own." She rushed back to her axe and quickly started to swing it back into the tunnel wall.

Blitzen's hefty form appeared in front of Charlie, blocking out his view from the rest of the mine. His muscles looked as if they wanted to burst through his skin. Charlie wasn't sure which was more intimidating—his stature or his beastly manner.

"I knew you'd be trouble," Blitzen grumbled. "You, thinking that you're better than everyone else."

In Charlie's peripheral, Zach used a shovel to pick up the coal he'd mined and dump it into a cart. Zach's mouth lifted up to one side as he turned back to his work.

"Take the cart," Blitzen said. "And follow me."

Tinkering with the top of his lamp, Charlie remembered what Rose had said about the dial, and only turned it a notch. Fire illuminated out in front of him like a mini blowtorch, highlighting a path. Charlie exhaled. That wasn't so bad.

The splintered, wooden cart sat before him on the rail track, with inky black pieces of coal piled inside. There weren't any handles for the cart, just the square frame and wheels connected to the track.

"You want me to push this… by myself?"

Charlie glanced around the mine, swallowing. He could see several other boys and girls pushing carts, but it took two or three of them pushing or pulling together, each of their faces strained and contorted. The cart had to be a couple hundred pounds, if not more, and the tracks were on a slight incline up to the conveyor.

"Impossible. I can't do that!"

Blitzen bared his teeth. "As punishment for not working, you will pick axe the coal with the rest of your team, and then you *alone* will push the cart up to the conveyor belt until further notice. If I see you slacking again, then I'll have you shovel the coal into the cart alone, too. Do you understand?"

Blitzen leaned in closer, and air from his nostrils puffed out into Charlie's face. "I said, do. You. Understand?"

"Y-Yes," Charlie said, stuttering.

"Good." Blitzen placed his hand on his whip and strode away, his massive form slowly disappearing from sight.

Charlie's heart pummeled as he stared into the darkness. He really was going to have to work down here in this mine. He sighed and peered back at his group. Rose looked over her shoulder and gave an apologetic shrug. Charlie's mouth flicked up in response.

Pressing his feet deep into the muddy ground, Charlie placed his hands on the chipped, wooden cart, and pushed. The cart squeaked and rolled an inch on the metal track. His arms shook and his muscles contracted. He dug his feet in harder into the earth, using the track's tie rails for leverage, fighting the cart's natural inclination to roll backward on him. The cart moved another inch, sweat dripping down his neck.

It was going to be a long afternoon.

If it *was* afternoon.

Charlie didn't know how long he'd been down there. Or how long any of them had been down there, for that matter. His teammates seemed to know so much already. It felt like it'd been days since the elves invaded his home and brought him here. It felt like it took hours for him to push the cart up to the conveyor belt and dump the coal onto the moving machine. It could've been years that he stood there pounding his axe and shoveling coal until he had to push the cart up to the conveyor belt once again.

His feet ached and his shoulders burned as he made his way back to his team for what seemed to be the hundredth time.

Charlie's breath came in and out in rasps, the air growing thicker with each movement. He pulled his pajama top away from his skin, trying to push off the stifling air. If he could just stop for a moment, then he'd be okay. But every time he paused, one of the reindeer guards would turn their gigantic racks of antlers toward him, tap their hands on their whips, and glare. Charlie would have to force himself onward, too afraid of adding another job to his regimen.

"You guys aren't much of a team," Charlie muttered as he returned from emptying the cart again. "You could've saved me from all this trouble."

"Sorry, Ches," Rose said, swinging her axe. "But this is the mine. You have to look out for yourself. We're not a family down here."

Zach barked out a laugh. His lamp shone in front of him, casting a yellow beam on the charcoal rock. "Seems like somebody's used to some pampering. Should I get you your binkie?"

"Nobody asked your opinion, Zach." Rose wiped the sweat off her forehead, smudging a long streak of dirt along her hairline.

Henry continued to mine silently off to the side.

"When does it stop?" Charlie asked. "I mean, are there ever any breaks? It seems like—"

"Noooooo...!" A voice echoed down the mine.

Charlie stiffened. "*What* was that?" he whispered to his teammates.

"Another one," Rose said. Her hand tightened on her axe, her knuckles white against her skin.

"Another one of *what*?"

"Taken down below. On the Permanent Naughty List now, just

like Timmy."

Zach grinned. "I wonder who's next."

Charlie leaned against the cavern wall, the rock cool against the back of his head. His hands trembled, and he stretched his fingers out stiff to steady them. The reindeer guards had wandered toward the commotion, so he felt okay about resting for a moment.

"You said that once you go down, no one has ever come back up," Charlie said. "What about those who... just get released? Can you just get put back on the Nice List?"

Rose let out a breath, blowing the whips of her auburn hair off of her face. "Well, sure, except that it's never happened before."

"*What*?"

"No one has never been put on the Nice List be—"

"I heard you. Why not?"

An air horn tooted through the mine, reverberating off the rocky walls and wood planks. Soft sighs sounded down the long tunnel, and the clanging stopped.

"Ugh. Finally!" Zach said, dropping his axe with a clank. "Food!"

9.

We all want some figgy pudding...

"Food?" Charlie's mouth dropped open. "You mean... we get to *eat*?"

Charlie grinned and excitement coupled with hunger bubbled in his stomach. He didn't think there would be any sort of comfort here. He didn't think they were going to feed him—that he was actually going to get a break from the endless digging and lifting and pushing. He was sure he was going to die from either exhaustion, heat, or starvation.

Out before him, a stream of lights had begun to form a straight line, rows of headlamps in the long, dark tunnel. The children faced away from the elevator, as if they were going to head deeper into the mine.

This was good, Charlie thought. He needed to know every inch of this place, and he had only seen a small portion of the perimeter.

"Come, on," Rose said. "If you're late, you won't get any food. *And* you'll be put on cleanup duty."

Charlie set down his axe and lined up with the rest of the kids.

With the sounds of the mining stopped, and the lamps all lined up in front of him, it felt strange to have complete silence and darkness on either side of him.

Blitzen's voice boomed from ahead. "Annnnd... *March! Left. Left. Left. Right. Left!*"

The children moved in sync, marching forward, lifting their knees, sharp and strong, moving like yellow ants in a black cave.

Charlie stumbled along the track, stepping on Zach's feet in front of him.

"Sorry," Charlie whispered.

"Watch it!" Zach said, spinning around.

The light from Zach's lamp blinded Charlie's eyes. Charlie stumbled again. Rose rammed into him, and Henry bumped into Rose. The three tumbled forward, making the line spill over like a row of dominoes.

Rose scrambled upward. "Get up, you guys! Charlie, you *cannot* get another punishment. Hurry!" She pulled Charlie to his feet.

Henry unfolded his thin frame, dusting off his footy pajamas, keeping his head lowered to the ground. Zach slowly stood, glaring.

Dasher and Dancer clopped up alongside the four of them, their black eyes pointed in their direction.

"What's the problem here?" Dasher growled.

"Who's out of line?" Dancer barked.

Zach opened his mouth, face smug, but Rose reached forward and nudged Zach between the ribs, stopping him from speaking. He scowled, but the three of them stayed silent.

"Blitzen will be interested to know a ruckus was caused here," Dasher said, pulling out his whip and giving it a loud crack. "Now march."

The children started the march down the long cavern again, into an area Charlie had never been before.

At the end of the mine, lit by a single torch, the tunnel split off into two directions, a pathway to the left and a pathway to the right. The children marched to the right.

Wet dirt continued to squish between Charlie's toes, thick and cool, until the ground became hard and dry. The hot, stale air was replaced by a warm, musky scent. The small dots of headlamps disappeared up ahead, swallowed up in a white, blinding light. Charlie blinked.

The tunnel came to an abrupt end and opened up into a large

room. Kids were turning off their lamps and removing their helmets, piling them outside the door. One by one, they filed inside the room, stepping past Blitzen, who narrowed his midnight eyes at each child as they passed.

As Charlie approached the room, he fumbled with the top of his lamp.

"Er... let me do that for you," Rose said, only half joking. "I'm not in the mood to have my head blown off."

Rose turned the dial on the top of Charlie's helmet, distinguishing the flame, and set their helmets down. Charlie threw her a thankful glance and moved forward, but as he stepped through the doorway, he could feel Blitzen's gaze shooting darts through the back of his head. He shivered, wondering what Blitzen's deal was.

Inside the room, long, metal tables stretched out before them, reaching one end of the room to the other. Bright, fluorescent lights buzzed overhead, giving off an unnatural glow. The lights made Charlie's eyes ache, and as he walked deeper into the space, he decided the lights were a torture of their own—he almost preferred the dark of the mine.

Boys and girls sat on cold, metal benches that were connected to the tables, with empty tin plates and cups out in front of them. Charlie kept himself glued to his teammates, not wanting to get separated from them. He remembered how Timmy got sent below from wandering too far off from his team.

The heavy, steal door to the room slammed closed with a bam. Blitzen stood in front of it, crossing his beefy arms. It was the first time Charlie had seen him in full light. The fur around his ears and snout were much more tangled and knotted, and his teeth had spots of decay. Scars were dug and cut into his arms and torso, and Charlie suddenly wished they were back in the dark.

Dasher, Dancer, and a couple of the other reindeer carried large, tin platters, the bottom half of their reindeer bodies squeezing through the aisles. They tossed the platters down onto the tables and the children dove in, hands flying inward.

Out before Charlie, lay a platter of cookies shaped like stars, trees, bulbs, angels, all covered in a variety of frostings and sprinkles.

Cookies!

Charlie's eyes widened as reached forward to grab one, but Zach swatted his hand away.

"Nope," Zach said, sitting across from him. "Newbies don't need sustenance. We've been here longer. Worked harder. Consider it… a donation." He chomped, chewing with his mouth open, gooey crumbs falling from his mouth.

Rose munched on her own cookie, licking the frosting off her fingers. She grabbed a pitcher, poured out a drink, and took a big swig from her cup. Charlie stared at her, waiting for her to come to his defense, but she only shrugged.

Charlie's stomach rumbled and ached. He glanced around the room, at the kids stuffing their faces full of frosted cookies, and then zoomed in on Zach's dark freckles and circular face. This wasn't fair. He shouldn't suffer just because Zach felt like torturing him. He hadn't done anything to him. If anyone deserved to be in this mine, it was Zach.

Charlie slumped. Maybe he wouldn't be okay after all. Maybe he wasn't going to get through this. Not with the heat, the work, the hunger, the kids, and the exhaustion. Not to mention the freaky elves and the reindeer. It really was one big nightmare.

Before him, a small hand slid a cookie across the table, and Charlie snapped his head up. Henry quickly drew his hand back, his curly mop of hair covered his slender face, and Charlie gave him a smile. The boy's eyes lifted, before they darted away.

Charlie picked up the cookie and took a bite. The familiar spiced flavor rolled around his tongue and burst into his mouth. Charlie gagged, spitting it out.

Gingerbread!

He reached for the tin cup in front of him and gulped down the liquid, frantic to wash away the flavor. He retched, and his stomach lurched.

Warm milk!

Charlie spit out the milk, spraying the liquid right into Zach's face.

Rose let out a quick chuckle.

Zach slammed his hands onto the table, his dark eyebrows digging into his forehead, his face screwing up tight. He sprung from his seat. Milk dripped from his hair, soaking his t-shirt.

"Oh, you are going to pay!" Zach said. He leapt over the table and grabbed Charlie by the shirt. He snatched a cookie from the platter and smashed it into Charlie's face, smearing frosting and sprinkles into his eyes and hair.

Charlie squirmed, trying to yank himself away, but Zach's hold was concrete. He glanced to the side, sure that Blitzen would intervene, but the beast only watched with humor in his eyes, a snarl on his hairy lips.

"Get... off!" Charlie tried to yell, but Zach was shoving cookie down his throat.

An air horn blared from outside, and the roomful of kids moaned. Dishes clinked and the tables creaked as kids stood from the benches.

Zach shoved Charlie backward.

Charlie crashed back into his seat, and Zach leaned forward.

"You're lucky this time, Ch... Ch... Ch... *Charlie...*" Zach whispered close to his ear. Charlie's eyes widened and his throat bobbed.

"Yeah, that's right. I know your real name." Zach grabbed Charlie's collar and turned it outward, exposing the name "Charlie" written neatly on the tag. "Looks like someone's mommy likes to put little Charlie Warlie's name on his clothes."

Charlie grabbed his shirt and pulled it tight against his neck, so that no one else could see.

"I wonder what Blitzen would do if he knew you lied to him. Should I tell him the truth? Get you sent to the Permanent Naughty List now? Or should I hold on to this information for a while? Hmm." Zach's face stretched into a malicious smile.

82

A loud whistle blew, and Blitzen's voice rang out, "Back to work!"

The kids quickly followed orders and began exiting the room.

Zach flicked Charlie in the middle of his forehead. "I think I'll hold onto this info for a while. See what I can get out of it."

"Chester!" Blitzen bellowed. "You're on cleanup!"

"Have fun cleaning, Chester," Zach teased, as he gulped down the rest of his milk. He burped right in Charlie's face, and walked off, chuckling.

"Man, can't you lay off the milk?" Rose said to Zach as she followed behind. She looked at Charlie and thumbed her hand towards Zach, pinching her nose, making a stinky face. "Lactose intolerant."

Charlie rubbed his neck, peering at the empty platters and bits of crumbs scattered on the tables. The fluorescent lights still buzzed overhead, ringing in his ears.

He glanced down at the unfinished cookie on his plate. In front of him, lay a little man with a green glob of frosting spread all over him. He stared for a moment, his eyebrows slowly drawing together, before he gasped. The vision of Emily picking up a green gingerbread man zoomed through his mind.

It looks just like the Grinch!

His sister's words echoed inside his head.

No.

It wasn't the same one he'd decorated at home. It couldn't be. He looked over the room again. Charlie had always wondered how Santa ate and drank all of the cookies and milk children left out for him on Christmas Eve.

Now he knew.

Santa didn't eat the cookies—he used them to feed the naughty kids who mined for the coal he delivered to the rest of the naughty children in the world. If kids knew that was what Santa was actually doing, Charlie was certain children wouldn't leave them out for Good Ol' Saint Nick anymore.

Charlie set to work, cleaning up the tables, and thought how he still didn't believe in Santa, but if Santa *were* real, he was worse than he had ever imagined.

10.

...the children were nestled, all snug in their beds...

Back in the mine, heat swirled around Charlie's head, tightening his throat. Sweat ran down his back in sheets, plastering his pajamas to his skin. For the umpteenth time, Charlie pushed the cart up to the conveyor belt, unloaded the coal, and watched the coal glide away. Again, he wondered where the coal went as the belt moved upward, disappearing into the mountain above him.

Charlie paused and swiped a hand over his face. He didn't understand why he was here.

Yes, he'd come to terms that this whole adventure wasn't a dream, and that a flying sleigh and elves had taken him here, and that the same Minotaur-like reindeer he'd drawn on Emily's picture existed, but it didn't mean *Santa* existed. It didn't mean he was *actually* digging for coal that would be delivered in stockings to naughty kids on Christmas Eve.

That was too much. He did have his limits.

But none of the reality before him made sense. Even if he did have a history of being a *tad* naughty, it didn't mean he deserved to be punished like this. And it didn't explain how the elves and freaky reindeer existed, and how all these other kids were here. Charlie wondered what they had done to get themselves here. He glanced around the mine, at the swinging pick axes. He needed to figure this out.

Charlie trudged back to his team. The ends of his pajama bottoms were ripped and soaking wet. His legs and feet ached and burned. His eyelids drooped, and the back of his head throbbed. He was convinced if he had to mine, load, and push the cart up to the conveyor one more time, he would die.

"There's the cart." Zach smiled with a knowing look in his eye. "Ow!" He dropped his axe and grabbed his thigh, feigning pain. "I think I have a *charlie* horse!"

Ignoring him, Charlie marched over to his spot on the mountain and started pounding his own axe into the rock.

"I don't think you heard me," Zach said. "I said, I have a *charlie horse* and need you to do my work for me. So, get over here and do it."

Charlie stopped, and stared Zach down, silence hanging between them.

"You'll get over it," Charlie responded.

Zach slowly bent down, picking up his axe. He analyzed the blade, before he drew his finger along the sharp tip.

"Do I need to call Blitzen over?" Zach threatened. "Let him know I have a *charlie* horse?"

Charlie tightened his fingers on his axe.

So this was how it was going to be. Zach *was* going to use Charlie's name against him—use the knowledge of his real name to squeeze out every bit of manual labor he could. It didn't make sense why Zach had such a beef with him.

He did *not* need this right now.

Charlie clenched his eyes shut, trying not to lose it. He thought back to Blitzen writing his fake name on the Naughty List. Charlie cursed himself for lying. He should've just been honest.

Peering open, Charlie grit his teeth, marched over, and started picking up Zach's mined coal and loading it into the cart. Zach gave a satisfied smile.

"What are you doing?" Rose hissed. "You shouldn't be doing Zach's work."

Charlie heaved out a breath. "I'm just... feeling... helpful."

Henry quietly worked off to the side, watching the proceedings with wide eyes.

After a few hours, another air horn sounded, and the mine seemed to exhale at once. Miners lined up along the rail track, some carbide lamps dimming a shade. Whips cracked, snapping down the shaft. Reindeer jotted up and down the long stretch of miners, barking out orders to stay in line.

"What's happening now?" Charlie whispered to Rose, as they lined up.

She turned and grinned, his dimming lamp highlighting the beauty mark by her right eye. "You'll see."

Charlie hefted his axe over his shoulder and marched with the kids down the mine. Instead of turning right at the end of the tunnel toward the dining hall, they went left. Charlie straightened his back, his head jerking side to side, taking in every detail. But like the rest of the tunnels, there was nothing of significance, no sign of escape, only jagged rock walls on either side of him.

Unlike the dining hall tunnel, there was no bright light up ahead, no large room waiting. Instead, the tunnel separated into a series of small nooks and alcoves, the walls morphing into crumbling dirt more than a solid rock. Children slowly separated and disappeared into their different nooks, hands rubbing their eyes, their mouths stretching into yawns.

With just the light of their fading lamps, Charlie followed Rose and Zach into a dusty alcove on the left, Henry just behind. Charlie ducked under the low ceiling, a few dried weeds sticking out from the broken earth.

Charlie's lamp spit and spattered, flickering out. He twisted the dial on the front, trying to give it more juice, but nothing happened.

"Don't bother," Rose said. "We only get so much calcium carbide a day, remember? When the flames go out, that's when the day is over. And we *finally* get to sleep."

"So… this is where we… sleep?" Charlie twisted his face.

"Yup."

"And… these are our… beds?"

"Yup. Choose a mattress." Rose leaned her axe against the dirt wall.

Four mattresses were strewn across the floor, all four of them had no sheets, no pillows—just bare, thin pads, stained with grime—but only one mattress had sharp, poky springs sticking up through the middle.

Charlie's eyes flicked to his teammates, and their eyes slid back to him.

They all stood frozen, staring at each other.

Charlie licked his lips.

Zack cracked his knuckles, and Rose and Henry tensed at the ready.

They all rushed forward at once.

Each diving for one of the good mattresses, Charlie sprinted from one bed to the next, but the others were too fast. Zach, Rose, and Henry parked themselves down, claiming the good beds before Charlie could reach them. Charlie wound up in the middle, circling.

"Ha!" Zach burst out laughing.

"Sorry," Rose said.

Henry's mouth turned downward, and his gaze skated away.

Charlie grunted and stomped over to the spiky mattress. He took off his helmet and scrubbed his matted, chestnut hair, flakes of dirt and rocks falling to the ground. He set down his axe and gingerly sat on the bed, avoiding the deadly coils poking through the thin pad.

The mattresses were positioned tight together, with only inches of walking space in between. With the ceiling low enough that Charlie could barely stand upright, and the walls just wide enough to fit the beds, stuffy air enclosed the area, squeezing in on Charlie's lungs.

Charlie lay back onto the pad and flinched. A sharp spring jabbed into his spine.

"Ow!"

Zach snickered off to the side.

Charlie shifted, maneuvering himself in between two sharp wires. He held still, not daring to move, in fear of getting poked again. He exhaled slowly, trying to relieve the aches and pains from the day, while trying not to create new ones from lying in an awkward position.

The other kids' lamps died out until the small alcove was completely dark. Some light seeped in from the single torch back in the entranceway, but just enough to see the how awful the sleeping conditions actually were.

Even though his eyelids were heavy, Charlie's eyes stayed wide open, staring at the dried weeds twisting through the dirt and rocks above him.

He needed to focus on what he was going to do about tomorrow. He couldn't keep going like this. This couldn't be how he'd live the rest of his life. This wasn't who he was—he didn't let others pick on him.

He had no control here, and he didn't like it.

He had no power over what he did, no power over who he was with. What he ate. Where he went. Blitzen was definitely out to get him —holding him up against the wall, threatening him, glaring at him like he wanted to eat him, and Charlie didn't see any of the *other* children doing extra tasks. On top of that, Zach had become a problem. Things were already bleak, and if his name was written on the Permanent Naughty List, and he was sent below, he wouldn't have any chance of escaping.

Charlie dug his fingertips into the sides of his temples and rubbed his head in circles. He tried to remember what he did at home when he was in trouble, and when he didn't get what he wanted—when his parents were ragging on him to do stuff and he needed to escape punishment—when he needed the attention off of him.

His mind spun, until he paused. He lowered his hands.

That was it.

He needed to get the attention off of him. He needed to do what he was best at.

He needed to be naughty.

Charlie had to make the other kids look naughty. He had to make

Blitzen and all of the other reindeer so busy and frazzled that they didn't have time to focus on him.

Just like he did with his parents.

If he could distract the reindeer from paying attention to him, then he could find an escape. He couldn't end up like Timmy.

A sour stench wafted through the air, interrupting Charlie's thoughts.

What was that?

The pungent smell hung in the stagnant air, settling into Charlie's nose. He coughed, waving the air in front of his face, sitting upright, gagging.

"I warned you," Rose mumbled from the mattress next to him. "Zach is lactose intolerant, remember? Why do you think I chose the bed farthest away from him?"

Charlie glanced over in Zach's direction. Through the dark, his breathing was slow and deep, his chest moving up and down in slumber. Another strange sound emitted from his body.

"Ugh!" Charlie lay back down, setting an elbow over his eyes.

Even little Henry squirmed on his bed, rustling.

"Good luck sleeping," Rose said.

Yeah. Charlie definitely needed to stir things up. He wouldn't last another night.

Tomorrow would be a new day.

11.

'Cuz I ain't been nothin' but bad...

The air horn blasted, but Charlie was already wide-awake.

He hadn't slept. Charlie had lain awake all night, staring into the jet-black cave, breathing in Zach's stench, ideas of escape whirling around in his head. The thought of being out of the mine soon made his body vibrate with anticipation.

His teammates groaned at the jarring sound, slowly rising out of their beds. Hoofs clopped in the tunnel outside, and torches flickered on the cave walls. Prancer and Vixen stuck their heads inside, yelling at the children to get up.

The kids each grabbed their pick axes and helmets and made their way out of the sleeping area. Charlie followed. The kids lined up in the main tunnel entrance, where Blitzen stood with a small, leather pouch tied around his waist. His large fingers dug into the bag and he divvied out two calcium carbide rocks to each child—their ration for the day.

Rose showed Charlie how to pop open the cylinder connected to

95

his helmet and set the two rocks inside.

"There you go," she said. "You're all set."

Charlie turned his dial two notches, then struck the flint mechanism. The flame burst to life, and the tunnel illuminated before him. Charlie blinked at the sudden brightness, and he marveled at the simple complexity of the contraption. He put on his helmet and peered down at his feet, cringing at the thick mud caked into his toenails. He'd never been one for personal hygiene, but this was too much.

"Should be a great day," Zach said, as he sauntered past, swinging his axe over his shoulder. "I have a feeling today won't be so bad. Not as much work as usual." His teeth gleamed under his own lamp.

"You know, I have the same feeling, too," Charlie said, straightening.

Zach's expression faltered, his eyebrows pinching together.

Soon, as if no time had passed since the day before, the pick axes swung up and down, the blades plummeting into the cold, hard mountain, the kids working like machines. Charlie suddenly wished he'd slept. His eyes started to burn, but he forced his eyelids open. He needed to stay alert.

It was almost time to bring his plan to fruition.

Charlie knew there wasn't an escape toward the dining hall and sleeping quarters, which meant he needed to go back toward the elevator if he were to find a way out. He remembered the big door he saw when he first arrived down in the mine, but without knowing what was behind it, Charlie quickly dismissed that option. There was the conveyer belt, but that was too risky—he couldn't ride up a moving belt without knowing where it went. The elevator was his only choice.

Charlie quickly finished loading the cart, then scrubbed his palms on his thighs.

"I've got this one," he told Henry, who gave Charlie a quizzical look.

"What?" Zach protested. "Why are you doing this creep's work? It's *his* day to push the cart."

Charlie ignored Zach and gave Henry a smile. Henry timidly smiled back, exposing the gap in his two front teeth.

Charlie began pushing the cart upward on the rail track.

As he pushed, he noticed the other kids didn't seem to be as miserable as him. Their faces were blank, not happy nor depressed, just... indifferent. Like they'd given up on ever getting out. Perhaps Rose was right when she said, *The mine breaks you one way or another.*

Charlie shook the thought away, he needed to stay focused and get the job done. That was how he lived his life. He always got what he wanted. As long as he kept his mind on the task, he'd be out of here and home, opening his *real* gifts before dinner.

Loud churning whooshed in his ears as he approached the conveyer belt. One by one, he picked up the pieces of the rough rock, and placed them on the moving belt. Charlie glanced to the elevator, then back to the moving rocks. His stomach wrenched.

If *one* thing went wrong and he was caught, then he was done.

"Enjoying your *break*?" Blitzen said, his breath tickling the back of Charlie's neck. "I've been watching you, Chester. Looking around at everything, thinking you're better than everyone."

He grabbed Charlie's shoulders and spun him around, so their faces were inches apart. "We. Don't. Stop. Working. Now move!"

Blitzen pushed him back.

Charlie stumbled away from the beast, gripping the cart. His fingers dug into the splintered wood, as Blitzen's massive form stared him down. Charlie glared back, then slowly turned away, dragging the cart back toward his team. He didn't have a choice but to continue with his plan. He never wanted to set eyes on Blitzen again.

"Hey, Chester. You okay?" Rose asked, as he drew near. "You seem... off."

Zach stopped mining and leaned up against the mountain. "Yeah, *Chester*." He lifted his brows.

Without a response, Charlie bit down onto his lower lip. He yanked a shovel off the wall and started shoveling the rocks into the cart as fast as he could, so much so that they spilled over the sides.

"And here I thought Henry was the weird one." Zach scoffed.

Henry, who was also watching Charlie with suspicion, looked away.

"Uh... Don't you think that's enough for this trip?" Rose asked Charlie.

Charlie stayed silent, knowing full well that the cart needed to be heavy enough for his plan to work. Charlie piled on a few more rocks and started to haul the cart back up the track.

It was time.

Charlie pushed and pulled, muscles straining. He kept his face forward, his jaw clamped down tight. He focused ahead, not daring to blink, and sucked in a shaky breath, forcing himself to exhale as he took in the reindeer's positions.

Charlie couldn't believe he'd had any hesitancy to escape before. This was what he was born to do.

Being naughty.

When Charlie got far enough up the track he stopped pushing and took a confident step out of the way.

Here we go.

The cart slowly started to roll backward, its rusty wheels squeaking under the weight. Squeak... squeak... squeak...

Charlie knew the cart was picking up momentum as the squeaks got closer together.

Squeaksqueaksqueaksqueaksqueak.

He could hear shouts of, "Look out!" and "Get out of the way!" before a...

Crash!

Chaos broke loose.

The entire reindeer guard rushed down the mine shaft to see what had caused the commotion. Shouts continued to echo, and hooves clopped. Charlie made a break for it, his legs eating up the ground.

He ran through the tunnel until the torch at the end of the mine came into sight. His chest soared. Charlie would be in the elevator and up to the surface before the reindeer would even know he was gone. His feet pounded faster. The elevator drew closer.

Everything was going according to plan until the elevator opened.

Blitzen emerged from the metal box and slammed the scissored gate closed behind him.

Charlie skidded to a stop. He leapt back into the dark, flattening himself against the cold, tunnel wall, breathing hard.

Blitzen moved into the tunnel, his eyes narrowed at the pandemonium. Charlie's throat burned. He was sure Blitzen had been in the mine. How could he have been so careless? He'd watched Blitzen all day, memorizing his routine. He hadn't accounted for possible trips to the elevator.

Charlie glanced down the shaft, at the frantic dark figures dashing about, listening to the screams reverberating back to him. He couldn't return now, but he couldn't move ahead, either. Charlie pressed deeper into the shadows.

Blitzen's huge frame strode further into the mine, stopping inches from Charlie, his gaze too fixed on the uproar to notice his location. Charlie's heart beat so fast he was sure Blitzen would hear it.

His mind screamed at him to run for his freedom, but his feet stayed rooted to the muddy floor.

Run for it.

But something in him couldn't. Blitzen might see him.

Just go.

Charlie crept toward the elevator. His feet met dry ground.

Hurry.

Blitzen still had his back to him.

Go.

He couldn't.

Now was not a time to lose confidence. He'd gotten this far. He was a few feet from his freedom.

"Got him!" a reindeer yelled from the darkness.

Charlie froze.

Got who?

Comet and Cupid dragged a small form forward. The boy walloped and kicked, his thin arms and legs flailing wildly.

"What is it?" Blitzen barked.

"We found the culprit," Comet said.

The two reindeer tugged the boy forward, a mop of sandy hair hanging over Henry's narrow face.

"His team's cart got loose and caused a big mess down there," Cupid said. "And it was *this* one's scheduled day to be pushing it."

Blitzen's hairy brows drew together. "Take him away," he ordered. "You know what to do with him."

"Henry—" Charlie choked, but the name came out in a whisper. "Henry!" Charlie tried again.

"Stop it!" Rose whispered, covering Charlie's mouth. She grabbed his elbow and yanked him backward into the tunnel. "There's nothing you can do for him now. We need to hurry. They're doing a headcount. You don't want to be missing."

"No. No!" Charlie tried to pry her long fingers off of him. "I'm not leaving him. It's my fault. My fault!"

Rose continued to pull Charlie deeper into the mine. The reindeer dragged Henry into the elevator, and Charlie continued to struggle.

"Henry!" Charlie yelled.

Henry's head snapped up, and his wide eyes met Charlie's just as the elevator gate closed. Their eyes stayed locked, until the elevator descended, disappearing with Henry into the darkness below.

12.

Do you see what I see...?

Days passed.

Or was it hours? Or weeks? Charlie wasn't sure anymore. Time seemed nonexistent. It was the same exhausting routine. Mine. Eat. Mine. Sleep. Repeat.

Charlie stared at the tunnel wall before him, the rock seeming to whirl around and around, falling inward like a never-ending black hole.

He recalled his stupid attempt to escape. He'd failed.

Not only had his plan failed, he'd failed Henry, too.

Charlie looked over the mine, at the tiny dots of lights and all of children swinging their axes. He wondered how many of them would end up underneath with Henry, never to see their families again. Probably all of them, if no one had ever made it onto the Nice List.

Charlie wondered if his parents missed him. If Emily missed him, even after all of the pranks and practical jokes he'd played on her through the years—or maybe his family was relieved he was gone.

Maybe a life without his naughtiness had made them breathe a sigh of relief. He could picture them now, feet up by the fire, sipping their hot cocoa, while Emily played peacefully with her new Christmas toys, no Charlie to ruin them.

And what about Henry's family? Would they feel the same way?

Charlie's stomach ached at the thought of Henry. The poor boy had never said a word to him, and yet Charlie knew he didn't deserve to be here. He was a good kid, and now, because of Charlie's stupid, selfish plan, he was gone forever, sent below, on the Permanent Naughty List, where he'd never be seen again.

Charlie rubbed a fist over his eyes, before he gripped his axe and turned back to the unrelenting mountain.

"It wasn't your fault, ya know," Rose whispered, setting her axe on the ground. "Bad things just happen sometimes. You can't stop it. You can only choose how you're going to move forward."

Charlie kept his mouth pressed shut, his eyes still frozen on the rock.

"It's not like you purposely let that mine cart go," Rose continued. "I know you wouldn't hurt him on purpose, Ches."

Charlie swallowed, but a lump lodged thick in his throat.

"No," Charlie answered, "I wouldn't."

"It's okay," she said. "Henry will be fine. He's a tough little guy."

"Really?" Charlie said, arms crossed. "Henry will be fine? He's a tough little guy. For what, the rest of his life? He's going to be fine underground all alone for the *rest of his life*? How can you not care?"

Rose lifted her thin brows, before they crunched together. "And why do *you* care?"

Charlie opened his mouth and paused.

"See?" Rose picked up her axe again. "I already told you. We're not a family down here. You have to look out for yourself."

"Well, maybe we should be," Charlie argued. "Maybe we need to stick together. Kinda like family's do, right? And families fight. But they have to trust each other, too."

This time, Rose paused. She tilted her head, as if chewing on the thought, before her eyes lifted to his. "Maybe you're right."

"Ugh!" Zach threw up his hands. "Don't believe him."

"And why not?" Rose demanded.

"Because he's a liar!"

"What?" Charlie glared at Zach.

Zach returned the glare and leaned in, and his voice lowered. "Because. You. Are. A. Liar."

"No. I'm. Not." Charlie ground his teeth.

Zach stuck his nose in closer. "Yes, you are."

"Prove it."

Charlie knew the minute the words escaped his lips he'd said the wrong thing.

Zach's face stretched wide, his eyes twinkling. "You want to know who our boy Chester *really* is?" he asked Rose. "He's been lying to us since the moment he got here. His name isn't really Chester. His name is *Charlie*."

Rose's head jerked over to him. Her eyes narrowed to slits.

"It's true," Zach continued. "Check the pajamas his *Mommy* made him."

Rose stared at Charlie, her mouth open, before she clamped her jaw down tight. She reached over and grabbed Charlie's collar, turning it outward. Rose quickly let go.

"Unbelievable!" Rose exclaimed.

Charlie moved his mouth, but no sound came out.

"Anything to say? Huh? *Charlie*?" Rose demanded.

Charlie shook his head. "I… I—"

Rose reached down and grabbed her axe and raised it high above her head.

Charlie stumbled backward, tripping over a pointy rock, catching himself against the cave wall. "Rose, please. I'm sorry. I didn't mean to hurt Henry. You have to believe me."

Rose started to swing the axe downward. Charlie clamped his eyes shut.

The axe plowed into the wall next to Charlie. Chunks of rock blew outward. Charlie's eyes shot open.

Rose raised her axe again.

"Rose," Charlie pleaded. "You have to believe me."

Rose swung the axe down again.

"Stick together?" she yelled as the axe dug deep into the wall again. More chunks of rock spit out.

"Rose, I'm sorry I lied."

Another swing. "Family?"

Rock flew everywhere.

The mountain shook with every blow. Bits of dirt and rock crumbled down from the ceiling above them, bouncing off their helmets.

The cage that hung overhead rocked, the dove flapping its wings violently.

"Rose, please!"

"Trust?"

Charlie watched as her swings became more vigorous. Her rhythm sped, her axe beating down harder, faster. The birdcage broke loose and crashed to the ground, releasing the dove inside. A series of rocks plummeted down.

"Rose!" Charlie yelled.

He pushed her out of the way as a cascade of rocks erupted, chunks of debris raining down. The wooden support beam groaned and splintered under the weight of the collapsing mountain, but was able to hold it from coming down completely.

Charlie dropped to his knees next to Rose, and he cleared the pile of rubble away. Rose coughed, her left leg scraped and raw.

"Are you okay?" he asked.

"What do you care?" Rose hissed. "Just go away." She pushed his hands aside and tried to get up, but fell back to the ground, her ankle twisted.

Footsteps approached, and Charlie knew without turning that

Blitzen had appeared behind them.

"Well, well, well..." Blitzen spoke. Charlie cringed. He hated being right.

"Chester McScrooge. Why am I not surprised to find you in the center of another disturbance?" Blitzen moved in closer. "What is the problem this time?"

"Problem?" Charlie stood up and dusted off his hands. "I'll tell you what the problem is. This place is this problem! Can't you see how dangerous it is down here? This whole ceiling could come down at any moment! What do you have to say about that?"

Blitzen took out his whip and cracked it close to Charlie's ear. Charlie didn't flinch. He kept his eyes locked on the beast, his chin lifted.

"Perhaps you should work more carefully," Blitzen said as he walked away. "But not too carefully," he called out, "you still have a quota to fill."

Charlie tightened every inch of his body, narrowing his eyes. He balled his fists and raced after the beast.

"Hey! You!" Charlie yelled, running up to him.

Blitzen paid no mind. He kept his antlers forward and continued up the tunnel.

"Are you kidding?" Charlie choked, trying to stop him, but Blitzen kept walking. Charlie jumped in front of him and shuffled backward. "We can barely see. We're barely fed. We hardly rest, and we work to the point until we can't stand."

Blitzen stopped at the end of the tunnel, where the door with the large lock sat to the left.

"Do you know how hard we've all worked?" Charlie threw out his hands. "We all deserve to go home!"

A deep rumbling came from Blitzen's chest. He moved in close until his breath was warm on Charlie's face.

"Unless your name is crossed *off* of the Naughty List and written *on* the Nice List in here," Blitzen pulled out the Naughty and Nice book, "you're not going anywhere."

Blitzen barked out a laugh, the sound booming off the cave walls. He stomped away, and disappeared behind the massive door, slamming it closed.

Charlie knew there was no way he was going to get his name on the Nice List.

It was impossible.

It didn't matter how good he was or how much work he did,

Blitzen would *never* write his name on the Nice List.

He might as well give up, hold out his wrists, and tell Blitzen to take him down to the Permanent Naughty List now, and lock him up until he was old and gray. His fate was already sealed.

Overhead, the freed dove from earlier circled, white and silent in the dark air, before landing on a small ledge on the wall high to the left. Charlie's forehead wrinkled. He moved up closer to the bird. It sat on a vent, the small grates of metal screwed into the cave wall.

He hadn't noticed the vent before. He had to know where the it led.

Charlie placed his palms on the cool tunnel wall, running his fingers over the sleek and rough spots. He didn't know if he could climb the wall up to the vent, but he had to try. The vent could be a way out.

Steady clangs and bangs sounded from down the mine, and Charlie glanced over his shoulder. No one approached. Inhaling deep, Charlie dug his bare toes and fingers into the grooves and crevices of the wall and pushed upward. His tendons strained and his stomach clenched.

Crossing one arm over the other, he climbed his way upward, arms shaking, sweat springing to his forehead. The rock bit into his fingers and toes, piercing his skin, but he forced himself onward, careful not to look down. The dove still sat above him, softly cooing, its white feathers almost glowing in the dark.

Charlie reached up, and his fingertips brushed the grate. His hands were slick, and he slipped, but he bent his legs, pressed his feet into the rock, and jumped, catching the vent. His fingers gripped the metal, and he pulled himself up.

He peeked through the grate.

Charlie saw Blitzen inside a small room. He moved about the tight space, grumbling to himself, before he fiddled with the keys on his belt. He removed the heavy set of keys and selected a large iron key, before unlocking a shiny vault in the corner.

The vault's door swung open, and Blitzen placed the Naughty and Nice book inside, before closing the vault again, locking it up tight. He returned the keys back safely onto his belt and squeezed his way over to a bed of hay on the other side of the room, plopping himself down with a huff.

Charlie fought to keep himself up on the wall, but the metal grate pierced his fingertips and his muscles strained. His fingers slipped, his hands disconnecting from the vent. He took one last look at Blitzen before he slid to the ground.

Charlie's thin frame hit hard on the dusty floor, and the dove took off into the black tunnel. Groaning, Charlie sat up, but his mouth pulled up into a half smile. He didn't know how, but he knew what he was going to do next. He was going to put his own name onto the Nice List.

13.

Tiny tots with their eyes all aglow,

will find it hard to sleep tonight…

Charlie lay on his bed, tapping his fingers over his stomach.

Rose had gone to sleep without a single word. Zach snored a mattress over, his putrid scent hanging in the air above Charlie's head. Charlie wrinkled his nose and rolled onto his side, one of the deadly mattress springs jabbing him into the shoulder. He couldn't bring himself to sleep on Henry's now vacated pad. It didn't seem right.

Charlie knew what he needed to do. He needed to wait until the mine was quiet and Blitzen was asleep, before he made his move. But too many questions ran through Charlie's brain.

If he succeeded in writing his name on *The Nice List*, would it work? Would he be freed? Or would the act itself put him on the *Permanent Naughty List* forever?

Charlie groaned, and rolled over onto his other side, wincing at another jab. He didn't need to worry about that now. He only needed to focus on one step at a time.

He reached up and started to bend the coiled piece of wire protruding by his face. He worked it back and forth until it finally snapped off. His mouth quirked up as he hid the pointy metal piece in his shirt pocket. It'd do the trick.

###

Charlie slid from his bed, and made his way out of the sleeping quarters, into the pitch-black tunnel. Dirt crumbled from the ceiling, and silence screamed in his ears. He took in a deep breath, stale air filling his lungs. Anything was better than the "Zach air" back in the alcove.

Charlie wished he had his helmet lamp, but he didn't have any calcium carbide left, and the light would be noticed for sure. Hopefully the repetition of walking up and down the mine shaft so many times would come in handy. Charlie opened his eyes as wide as they would go —hoping he could see a little—making his way down the tunnels.

He ran a hand along the bumpy wall, his fingers gliding along the smooth and rough surface. He counted his steps, noting in his memory where he was. His teams' mining area. The spot where Henry's cart had crashed. The KEEP OUT danger zone.

Charlie tried not to think about what would happen if he got caught—so he pushed himself forward, his feet slowly swallowing up the dark distance in front of him.

It seemed like forever when he finally approached the end of the tunnel. The elevator came into view, barely lit by the torch on the wall next to it. Charlie blinked, trying to get used to the flickering light. The conveyor was still and silent. He drew to a stop, listening, then turned to the heavy wooden door to Blitzen's office.

Charlie crept forward, his breath high in his chest.

The torch cast a dull glow, shadows dancing over the door. Kneeling down, he removed the pointy wire he'd tucked into his pajama top and stuck the metal into the keyhole.

Charlie recalled the decorative antique keys in all of the doors at home—all of the doors except for Emily's. His mom had thought it would keep him from getting into her room and cutting the hair off of her Barbie dolls. It had worked for about a day. Then he'd learned on the internet how to pick a lock. Those poor dolls.

Charlie's heart dropped at the memory, but he set back to work.

After wiggling the wire for a moment, the lock unlatched with a clink. Charlie paused, listening again. He rose, and carefully turned the iron knob, pushing the door open. The hinges creaked, and Charlie winced.

He listened again.

A sliver of light sliced through the dark room as Charlie slipped inside. He closed the door, and it clicked.

To the right, a large, ornate pedestal sat next to the vault, and to the left, Blitzen was fast asleep on a bed of hay. Diamonds of light came through the vent and fell over Blitzen, casting sinister shadows on his face.

Charlie inched his way to the safe, the floors as smooth and hard as the rock walls around him. With the bent piece of wire in hand, Charlie slid the metal into the keyhole of the vault. He fiddled and twisted, but the lock wouldn't open. Charlie screwed up his face, trying again, but it wouldn't budge. He glanced to Blitzen, hands shaking, and tried again.

Nothing.

Charlie's palms grew slick, and his pulse sped.

Why wouldn't it open?

Charlie's eyes slid over Blitzen's sleeping form—over his muscles and scars, down to the keys hanging from his belt.

Charlie inwardly sighed, wanting to stamp his foot.

This wasn't happening.

Charlie shook his head, and tiptoed over to the beast, resisting the urge to close his eyes. He approached Blitzen's bed, and a piece of hay crunched under his feet. Charlie sucked in a breath, waiting, but Blitzen stayed asleep. Charlie took another step. The hay crunched again. Charlie paused. Nothing again. Charlie took another step.

Finally, Charlie reached forward, and his fingers connected with the heavy keys. He wrapped his fingers around the loose keys to prevent them from jingling. Charlie bit his cheek, not daring to breath, and lifted them from the belt.

Blitzen snorted, and his eyes flew open.

Charlie reacted on instinct.

Charlie reached down and scratched Blitzen behind the ear. Back home, it had worked on Fluffy, maybe it would work on Blitzen, too. The coarse hairs under Charlie's fingers made his stomach turn. Charlie shrunk back, making a face, until he relaxed. Blitzen's eyelids closed. Charlie held still, until he inched backward with the keys.

Charlie slid a brass key into the safe's lock. Its internal mechanism clicked, and Charlie's heart jumped when the door swung open, revealing The Naughty and Nice Book.

Charlie hefted the book upward and set it down onto the pedestal. He traced his hand along the leather casing, over the carved pictures and symbols, his fingers digging into the smooth grooves and bumps. He carefully opened the book.

The binding crackled, and the smell of old paper filled Charlie's nostrils, reminding him why he hated going to the library. On the page before him, *The Naughty List* was written in an elaborate, elegant scrawl.

Charlie's chest tightened.

He turned the pages, eyes frantically scanning down the list of names.

Clarke, Davis

Christensen, Fawn

Cooper, Melvin

He scanned down the next page. No Charlie.

What?

Oh.

Last name!

Charlie flipped to the last names that started with the letter P, but there was no Peters.

What?

122

Oh, duh!!!

Charlie had forgotten that he'd given Blitzen a fake name. He flipped back through the pages to the letter M.

He ran his finger down the list of last names.

McScrooge, Chester!

Yes!!

Charlie snatched a feathered quill off the wooden desk and dipped it into the pot of ink to his right. A drop of ink plopped onto the table.

Ugh. Black.

It used to be Charlie's favorite color, but in that moment, he promised himself that he'd *never* wear black again.

Charlie zoomed back in on his fake name and crossed it out. He even scribbled it out a second time for extra measure. Charlie flipped the book over and searched for the section that read, *The Nice List*. He found the "P" section and sweat sprung to his forehead.

Charlie stopped.

He stared at the page—at the empty spot at the bottom of the list. He'd waited for this moment since he got here.

He was *finally* going to get his name on *The Nice List*.

Charlie closed his eyes. He breathed in and waited for his heart to slow. His hand trembled, and he lowered the pen to the yellowed paper.

Charlie wondered what would happen after he wrote his name down. He wondered if he'd magically be whisked away back to his house. If the elves would trickle in and take him up to the sleigh.

A shadow came up from behind, darkening the page before him. Charlie's head shot up, and he dropped the pen.

"Tsk tsk tsk," a gruff voice said.

Charlie stiffened, and slowly spun around.

Blitzen stood with his whip out, and his large antlers nearly touching the ceiling.

"Now you've really made a mess of things," Blitzen said. "I hoped it wouldn't come to this, but things are beyond my control now. Looks like we'll have to take you to see the man himself. And he *won't* be happy."

14.

He knew in a moment it must be Saint Nick…

Charlie took off.

Ducking underneath Blitzen's beefy arm, he sprinted towards the office door, and dove for the door handle. Charlie's fingers skimmed the knob, but Blitzen caught him by the collar, dragging him backwards. Charlie kicked the beast's legs, but Blitzen didn't flinch. Charlie battered and thrashed, but Blitzen held him secure.

"Get off!" Charlie yelled. "Let me go!"

Blitzen growled, and snatched the book. He stomped over to the door and yanked it open. Charlie continued to fight. He elbowed Blitzen in the gut. He tried to turn and bite his hand, but Blitzen's hold was too tight.

Charlie's thoughts spun.

He had to get away. He remembered one time when Emily had grabbed his t-shirt after he'd stolen one of her toys, and he was trying to escape. Charlie had slipped the t-shirt off over his head. He wondered if the same trick would work now. With his arms raised, Charlie dropped like a bag of sand. Hot air hit his bare skin, and Charlie shook his head, dazed.

It worked!

Free, Charlie raced for the elevator, Blitzen's footsteps charging behind. Charlie slid the gate open, leapt inside, and slammed the gate closed. Charlie's breaths burst in and out, and his arms and legs shook. Charlie gripped the red lever hard and wrenched upward.

Blitzen's massive form came plowing forward, and his antlers rammed into the gate.

The elevator's gears churned, and it began to ascend.

Blitzen punched the gate as he watched Charlie move upward, his teeth bared, his black eyes unmoving.

Charlie grinned as Blitzen's form disappeared below. The elevator rose, and Charlie looked upward, toward his freedom. Now he just needed to make his way to the sleigh.

###

The elevator lurched, and the lever popped back into its neutral position. The gate swung open, and Charlie's brows dug together.

An elf stood waiting, his face smug, his arm extended,

welcoming Charlie outside.

The elf was a stark contrast to the elves below, with his breeches and sackcloth shirt untouched from soot.

"End of the line," the elf said, his voice gruff.

Charlie gasped and quickly gripped the lever, shoving it upward. The elevator didn't move. Charlie shook the lever up and down, kicking the box with his feet.

"Come, on. Move!" he yelled.

The elf tapped his foot.

Charlie yanked the bar again, groaning through his teeth. The elevator still wouldn't budge. Charlie gave the metal box one last kick.

"Are you finished?" the elf asked. "Because he's expecting you."

Charlie stopped.

"He?" Charlie asked. "Who's… he?"

The elf's wrinkled face pulled up into confusion. "Who else?"

Charlie fiddled with the lever again. It still wouldn't budge.

The elf's sharp teeth poked out from his upper lip, and his eyes twinkled. "It won't work," he said. "You have no choice. You're *going* to visit him."

Charlie slowly lowered his hands as the elf motioned him outside again.

"This way."

Charlie hugged himself as he followed the elf.

The area immediately opened up into a large space, dark, but lit by torches on the rock walls. Charlie felt a cool breeze drift over his face, and chills rippled along his arms. He wasn't in the mines anymore. Familiarity tickled along the back of his neck. From the corner of his eye, red flashed and his eyes widened.

The sleigh!

He was back in the cave!

Charlie's fingers flexed and his scrubbed his palms on his pajamas. His eyes darted between the large vehicle and the elf.

"Keep up," the elf said. "He sees all. He knows all."

Charlie swallowed, keeping his eyes on the sleigh, until the elf led him to the tunnel where Charlie had first met Blitzen.

Golden bulbs lit the path straight ahead, some burned out, some flickering, and some buzzing too bright, highlighting cobwebs dangling from the ceiling. Charlie glanced behind him, hoping to catch sight of the sleigh once more, but there was nothing, just the golden orbs around him.

At the end of the hall, a gigantic steel door was bolted into sparkling rock. Next to the door, a control panel was screwed into the rock, a series of buttons and flashing lights on the front.

The elf's gnarled hand reached up and punched in a code. Charlie wished he'd memorized the code, but there were too many numbers—twenty-five at least—and the elf's long fingers had moved too fast. The door clicked and beeped, and the elf twisted the handle.

The door swung open.

"In," the elf demanded.

Charlie obeyed.

The room inside was the size of a warehouse—three times bigger than his home—and concrete from top to bottom. In the middle, a single spotlight shone down, highlighting a large wooden chair, with a small, circular table sitting adjacent. It was empty, save for a single feathered quill. In the front sat a wooden stool.

On the far side of the room, a stone archway stretched from ceiling to floor. Black tinsel hung from the rock, with drooping, dead Holly Berries. Underneath the archway, was another door with a tarnished brass doorknob, shaped like a Christmas tree. Charlie wondered who or what would need a door that large.

To the right, a machine was connected to the wall. The conveyor belt stuck out from the opening and terminated three feet from the machine. Just below, were several large piles of coal.

Charlie's eyebrows shot upward.

This is where the coal went.

He wondered how much coal was produced a day, and how many kids found a hard lump in their stockings on Christmas morning.

To the left, tables extended from one end of the room to the other, where a myriad of scattered weapons and trinkets lay. Charlie squinted, trying to see what was on the tables in detail, but it was hard to see.

"What is this place?" Charlie's voice bounced off the empty walls.

The elf only smiled.

Blitzen barged into the room, the door hitting the opposite wall, the Naughty and Nice Book wedged into the crook of his arm. His veins bulged from his skin, and one hand clutched Charlie's pajama top.

"You. Sit. Now," Blitzen barked. He pointed to the stool.

Charlie backed away. "But—"

Blitzen threw Charlie's pajama top into his face. "Santa is on his way. And boy, is he angry."

Blitzen clomped to the middle of the warehouse and tossed the book onto the table. The spotlight shone down on his face, darkening his eyes.

Charlie gingerly sat down. He pulled his shirt back over his head and placed his hands on the top of his thighs. Santa? Was coming to see him? *Now?*

"I wouldn't be surprised if this is the last time I see you," Blitzen said. "And good riddance."

Blitzen kicked the leg of Charlie's stool, tipping it, sneering as Charlie crashed to the cement floor. Blitzen and the elf marched from the room, Blitzen's laughter booming down the hallway until the door shut tight.

Charlie glared, rubbing his elbow. He hoped he *never* saw Blitzen again. He picked up the stool and sat back down.

Charlie stared at the door, waiting.

Waiting.

Waiting.

For never believing in Santa, the man certainly frightened Charlie.

Finally, Charlie hopped off the stool and crept over to the tables.

He peeked behind him, and ran his hand along the dusty surface, taking in the knickknacks.

There were whips. Carved knifes. Slingshots. Music boxes. Whittled figurines and animal skins. Charlie sifted through, picking up random items, and setting them down. Doll heads. Lonely puzzle pieces. Springs.

A bag of marbles.

Charlie smiled, and picked up the small, leather pouch. He dug his fingers inside, and pulled out a clear glass sphere, holding it up. Inside, vanes of orange and red swirled with a hint of black. A Cat's Eye. It was rare to find a marble with a black swirl inside. Charlie had always wanted one of these.

"Find something you like?"

Charlie jerked, dropping the bag of marbles, and spun around.

In the doorway, the man before him was much bigger than Blitzen, not only in length, but in width. A huge set of ram-like horns curled out from his head, scraping the top of the archway as he ducked inside.

Charlie's mouth fell open.

This definitely wasn't the Santa from Emily's books.

No red and white coat. No rosy cheeks and joyful smile. No snowy beard. Instead, his coat was brown, with splotches of dirt and grime, and spots that looked like they were growing fungus. His cheeks were chapped and dry, and his smile was crooked, filled with greenish-yellow teeth. His beard was blackened with coal dust.

The only word that escaped Charlie's mouth was a barely audible, *Krampus*.

Santa's bloodshot eyes stayed flat as he calmly strode forward. He was next to Charlie in a couple strides.

"Krampus. Santa Claus. Saint Nicholas. Call me what you will, but one thing is for sure..." The top part of his body seemed to bend in half as he leaned down and looked Charlie in the eye. "I am real."

Charlie leaned away. His breath stank of sleep and sour milk. His beard littered with gingerbread crumbs.

Santa's large hand slowly lifted, pointing to the stool. He stared at Charlie, not saying a word, his finger outstretched. Charlie edged towards the stool, somehow knowing if he didn't obey, there'd be big consequences.

"Ah, there it is," Santa said. "The Naughty and Nice Book." He picked up the book and ran a hand on the binding. "Carved these symbols myself. Impressive, aren't they?"

Charlie kept his mouth closed tight.

Santa slammed the book down onto the table. "Aren't they?"

Charlie nodded. "Y-Yes. They are, Santa, S-Sir." He remembered how his Dad liked to be called "Sir" when he was angry.

Santa pressed his chapped lips together. He spread both hands over the front of his rusted coat. Santa lowered his body into the large chair. It groaned under his weight. Even though Santa was sitting, Charlie still had to strain his neck to look up at him.

"Now, about your actions," he said. "Sneaking out of bed. Breaking into Blitzen's office. Trying to write your name on the Nice List. In all my years, I've *never* had a kid perpetrate such brazen acts. What do you have to say for yourself—" Santa's eyes narrowed, "Charlie Peters?"

Charlie blinked, and his cheeks flushed. How did Santa know his name? Had Zach snitched on him?

"You forget, I am Santa Claus," Santa reminded him. "I see you when you're sleeping. I know when you're awake." He laughed an evil laugh.

Charlie tightened his eyes and leaned forward. "I'll tell you what

134

I have to say for myself," he said, voice low. "What's the deal with you *never* putting any of the kids back on the Nice List, huh? What do *you* have to say about that?"

Santa peered at Charlie, frozen in thought. His mangled brows drew together, his hand pulling on his beard. Crumbs fell from the tangled mess.

"You're right," Santa finally said. "I have never put a kid back on the Nice List. And if anyone deserves to have their name there, it's *you*, Charlie."

Charlie straightened, and his pulse leapt. "You mean it? I can go *home*?"

Santa nodded. He picked up the Naughty and Nice Book and grabbed the feathered quill.

"I can do it right now, if you'd like. You'll be home opening presents, eating warm food, and sleeping in your own bed in a jiffy," he said. "However, if I write a name on the Nice List, it has to be replaced by another name."

Charlie jumped up from his seat. "Fine. I don't care. Do it! I want to go home!"

"Are you sure?" In order to keep the balance of the mines, you'll have to choose a name from the Nice List who will replace you."

Charlie stopped. "What? Me? I have to choose a name?"

"Don't worry. It will be random, but yes."

Charlie's heart dropped. Someone had to replace him. He didn't think someone from the Nice List had to be removed, but he was desperate to go home. He'd spent enough time down here—and he wouldn't know who this person was. Why should he care? Besides, if *he* had found a way out, other kids would, too. Who was to say this person wouldn't?

"So what will it be, then?" Santa asked.

"I... I want to go home," Charlie said, squaring his shoulders.

"Home it is." The blood red veins in Santa's eyes darkened, and he lifted the pen to the book. With great care, Santa elegantly wrote Charlie's *correct* name on the page.

Charlie watched as Santa finished. He felt the tension drain from him.

He'd done it.

He was free.

Finally, he was going home. His hands tingled, and his mouth relaxed into a smile.

"Alright, and for your replacement," Santa said. "Close your eyes and point to a name."

Sweat gathered on his forehead, but Charlie wiped it away, and swallowed.

"Okay."

Taking a deep breath, Charlie shut his eyes. As Santa opened the book to the Nice List, Charlie reached up, and pointed.

He opened one eye, and blanched.

"What? No!" Charlie said, shaking his head. "This can't be! No!"

A cruel smile spread along Santa's pot-marked face.

Right under Charlie's finger, written in a neat scrawl, was the name, *Emily Peters.*

15.

Oh, the weather outside is frightful…

"You tricked me."

Charlie stared up at Santa, mouth parted, pain throbbing in the back of his throat. "You can't… this is unfair. You… you tricked me!"

"Blitzen!" Santa boomed, smiling down at Charlie. "Prepare the sleigh. I'm going to go get this new recruit *myself*."

"No!" Charlie yelled, his fingers tightening into his palms. "You can't. Not Emily. Anyone but Emily!"

Blitzen bolted from the room and then quickly returned. "While the sleigh is being prepared, is there anything else?"

"He's free to go," Santa said, flicking his hand outward. "Time to give a little boy everything on his wish list." He winked, and a glint of light seared along his horns. "Escort him from the mine."

Blitzen's lips curled and a smile stretched over his face. "With pleasure."

"No! No!" Charlie yelled again.

Everything happened too fast.

Two elves scampered forward. Strong hands gripped his arms. Charlie was pulled across the warehouse, his heels dragging on the cold, cement floor. The bells on the elves' shoes sounded far away, distant in the back of Charlie's mind. The air moved past his face, his mind in a numb haze.

"Oh, Charlie?" Santa called.

Charlie turned his head.

"I'll take good care of Emily." His rotted teeth flashed. "I promise."

Charlie's stomach sunk as he was shoved from the room. He followed Blitzen and the two elves along the sparkled hallway with the golden globes. They passed the sleigh where a group of elves hustled and bustled preparing it for Santa and headed toward the elevator.

"Where are you taking me?" Charlie asked, voice dry. "I thought I was free."

"Not yet," Blitzen said, lips curled.

They boarded the elevator, and Blitzen lowered the red lever. The elevator groaned, dropping downward, back toward the mine. The elevator drew to a stop, and the familiar stale air hit Charlie's face as they moved into the tunnel.

"Sound the horn," Blitzen barked to the two elves. They skittered away, nodding.

Charlie shook his head, still in a daze. He couldn't break out of it. Somewhere in the back of his mind, he knew he was in shock.

Kids yawned as they emerged from the sleeping quarters. They marched around the corner into the long tunnel, eyelids drooped.

Blitzen waited, lips still curled, until the children stopped in front of him.

"Your sleep was interrupted because we have an important announcement," Blitzen said. His voice echoed down the length of the mine. "Charlie, why don't you give your peers the exciting news."

Charlie glanced up at Blitzen, the daze finally broken. "W-What?"

"Your news. Give it to them."

"My news? You mean...? No. That's insane. I'm not giving it them."

Blitzen bent down, his antlers hovering over him. "Give it to them. Or I'll tell Santa you disobeyed, and I'm sure he'll have special consequences for Emily."

Charlie recoiled back and peered over at the sleepy kids. Pain throbbed behind his eyes.

"Fine," he said.

Charlie rubbed the back of his neck and cleared his throat.

"I-I've been set free," he said. "I'm back on the Nice List."

Gasps burst through the mine. Whispers traveled from kid to kid.

"Is that all you have to say?" Blitzen raised a hairy brow.

Charlie's eyes stretched wide.

"What Charlie *means* to say is that he *cheated* his way onto the Nice List." Blitzen puffed out his chest. "And because he cheated the system, all you miners will now have to work twice as hard as you are now. Meaning, thanks to Charlie, you are now required to mine twice the amount of coal in the same amount of time. Or you will be punished. Severely."

Blitzen took out his whip and cracked it, the sound jolting the kids awake. "Starting now."

Moans exploded down the mine and glares shot in Charlie's direction. Words like, "Unbelievable" and "Selfish" were mumbled as the kids departed.

Zach brushed past him. "Thanks a lot, dude. Rose was right. We can't trust each other."

He nudged Charlie's shoulder hard as he walked away again.

Charlie stepped forward. "Zach, wait. I'm—"

"Don't," Zach said. "Just don't."

Rose stood off to the side, her arms crossed.

Charlie's throat bobbed.

Blitzen trotted up and stomped his hooves. "Get to work!"

"Have fun with your *freedom*," Rose said and stomped away. She threw one last glare over her shoulder, before she disappeared into the dark.

The elves pushed Charlie back into the elevator. Blitzen squeezed himself in next to him, pressing Charlie flat against the metal wall. He smiled down at Charlie as he closed the scissor gate slowly, purposefully. The latch closed softly with a click.

Charlie watched as the kids started mining, hefting their axes up and down, with a renewed, but reluctant fervor. Charlie dropped his eyes, but the sounds of splitting rock screeched inside his head. He covered his ears, but the sounds wouldn't stop.

"Proud of yourself?" Blitzen asked as the elevator rose. "I bet you thought one little choice wouldn't affect so many people. Not that I mind. Twice as fun for me." His eyes gleamed.

Charlie's throat felt swollen. First he'd ruined Henry's life, then Emily's, and now... look what he'd done to all of those kids. They were going to suffer for the rest of their lives because of him. They didn't deserve this. None of them did. Charlie lowered his head and pinched the bridge of his nose.

The elevator bounced to a stop, and they all exited.

The elves led Charlie back to where they continued to prepare Santa's sleigh.

All of the other reindeer were also there, strapping themselves two by two into the harnesses that were connected to the neck yolks and single trees. There was Dasher and Dancer and Prancer and Vixen. Comet and Cupid and Donder and—

Blitzen broke away from Charlie and clopped over to the sleigh. He positioned himself next to Donder at the front of the team. Charlie wondered why the reindeer needed to travel with the sleigh if the sleigh had the capability of flying by itself—but then he remembered what the elf said on his trip to the North Pole. The reindeer were all part of Santa's "image."

As if on cue, Santa emerged from the tunnel. He ignored Charlie, and lumbered over to the sleigh, and stepped inside. He sat down with a grunt, his weight causing the sled to lower a few inches on its skids.

An elf scurried up to the sleigh, holding a vile of red, swirling liquid. On the side of the sleigh, he removed a cap from a nozzle that protruded from the vehicle. He poured the thick liquid into the nozzle, and it took a while to make its way into the sleigh, as the red liquid gooped in like syrup. Charlie scratched his head, wondering what the liquid could be. It must've been what gave the sleigh its ability to fly.

A different elf approached Blitzen and handed him another vile of the same substance.

Blitzen brought the vile to his lips, and downed red liquid. He tossed the empty vile back to the elf and wiped his mouth.

"You know what to do with the boy," Blitzen ordered the elves. "Throw him outside." His mouth curved up at Charlie.

"What?" Charlie asked. "You're not... you're not going to... take me with you? How will I get home?"

"That's not my problem," Blitzen said, as he tightened the harness close his body. "You should have thought about that before you tried to fool Santa. But no, you're too selfish to think things through."

"But... I'm just a boy!"

"A boy who will never change."

Charlie opened his mouth, but he choked on his own response.

Blitzen shook his head. "You're free aren't you? Isn't this exactly what you wanted?"

Before Charlie could respond, Santa grabbed the reins and gave them a quick crack. The reindeer all snapped to attention, and simultaneously began pulling the sleigh. At first, they struggled to pull its weight, but they got traction and moved the vehicle towards the cave exit. Faster and faster they sprinted, and then, as if by magic, the sleigh and the reindeer lifted off the ground.

And just like that, it drove out of sight.

Charlie stood there, dumbfounded.

Despite his current situation, Charlie couldn't help but marvel at what had just happened. He'd seen a lot of things in Santa's mine, but this, by far, was the most impressive.

Tiny hands dug into Charlie's arms.

"Let's go."

16.

And if you ever saw it...

Two elves led Charlie toward the cave opening where Santa and the sleigh had just exited. Wind whistled outside, and clouds stretched over the moon like cotton candy.

The elves jerked Charlie to the right, away from the opening into a tunnel Charlie hadn't noticed before—it headed downward at a sharp incline, into the mountain. Two more elves joined the party, and they flanked Charlie on either side.

The air warmed as the wind disappeared, and darkness closed in as they descended through the tunnel, winding left and right. They walked in silence for what seemed like an eternity. Charlie kept his eyes locked on the path before him. Finally, the stale air gave way to a chilling, dry air.

Charlie's teeth chattered as the elves pushed him forward down the rocky, narrow passageway. Ahead, beyond a black iron gate, the wind whipped up white snow, whirling and surging in all directions against the night sky. The landscape was a flat, frozen tundra save for a single frosted red and white striped pole sticking up from the ground, standing firm against the unrelenting storm.

A large gust of snow billowed in through the gate, leaving pellets of frozen water on Charlie's eyebrows and lashes. Charlie rubbed his arms, the sweat on his forehead suddenly gone.

The elves pushed Charlie close to the gate, their hold on him tight. Snow and ice had drifted under the gate, a layer reaching up to Charlie's ankles, his bare feet and toes starting to go numb. The mass of gray clouds were severe against the black sky, the wind moving them fast.

One elf removed a set of keys from his belt, the keys engulfing his small hands. The elf's wrinkled lips pinched as he sifted through the options, and picked one large, iron key, bringing it close to the gate lock.

"Aw, do we have to throw him out?" one elf asked, breaking the silence. "Can't we just keep him to ourselves? Keep him as a snack?" he licked his lips and stared down at Charlie's toes. The other two elves' eyes twinkled red and nodded in happy agreement.

"Sorry, mate," the elf with the keys answered, "but as delicious as that sounds, orders are orders."

The other three elves sagged. One kicked a tuft of snow.

Charlie tried to back away.

"You don't have to listen to Blitzen, you know," Charlie said to the head elf. "He isn't the boss of you."

The elf's lips twitched. "Who said anything about Blitzen? We know who knows all. Sees all." The elf reached up and pushed the key into the lock.

Charlie shut his eyes. He couldn't leave. Not with Emily coming. He had to stay. He couldn't leave Henry and Rose and Zach and all of the other kids. He couldn't leave them to their fate because of him. His chin quivered, but he clamped his mouth down tight.

There were four elves surrounding him. Only two held him secure.

He quickly calculated that with all of the reindeer gone, there were only the elves left to contend with. His chances were pretty good. He could do this. He could escape.

The elf turned the lock.

It was now or never.

He opened his eyes.

Charlie stomped down on one elf's foot and kneed another in the stomach. He yanked one elf's arm down as hard as it would go. The elf's grip loosened, and he cried out. Charlie shoved the last elf into the other three. They tried to brace themselves, but couldn't get their footing, and they slipped into the snow drift. They all fell down like a house of cards.

Charlie took his chance and raced back through the tunnel. His footsteps were muted in the narrow passageway, the cold stinging his cheeks.

"You won't get far!" one of the elves shouted.

Charlie pushed his way up the winding tunnel and into the cave without even hearing the elves behind him. He reached the elevator, rammed the gate closed, and wrenched the lever down.

The elevator lurched downward and stopped on the mine level. Charlie knew he didn't have much time before Santa and the reindeer guard returned. He had to do something and do it quick. He couldn't do this on his own. He needed help.

Without a helmet, Charlie rushed through a pitch-black tunnel, dragging his hand along the bumpy wall, water splashing around his ankles, making his way through the maze-like shafts of the mine toward the miners.

"Check down there!" a raspy voice yelled.

"And I'll look down here!" another gruff voice said.

Elven voices ricocheted off the walls. They'd been alerted to his escape.

Charlie figured all of the elves would be after him by now. He wasn't sure how many that would entail, but now that he thought about it, he'd seen so few elves the whole time he'd been trapped down here—maybe ten total—which didn't make sense. He thought Santa would have at least fifty elves in his workshop. But he needed to get to his teammates. He was sure he could reach his destination before—

Charlie stopped in his tracks.

Two elongated shadows stretched on the tunnel ahead, followed by voices behind. He hovered in the main shaft, weight bouncing, his gaze darting from space to space. He took in the work stations, the carts, the piles of half-stacked coal, and... the blocked off tunnel with the DANGER and DO NOT ENTER signs.

He reacted on instinct.

Charlie dove into the darkness, into the forbidden tunnel. The ground dipped at a sharp incline, and goose bumps prickled his skin. A wooden beam creaked above him, groaning, and he wondered if that was why this tunnel was off limits. This tunnel could collapse at any moment.

Voices echoed, and more shadows elongated on the wall behind him.

Charlie pressed himself against the rock wall, and he inhaled, holding his breath. The elves passed by him, unaware that Charlie was only a few feet away. Charlie heard the elevator stop and the familiar sound of the screeching gate. A few voices shouted, and then he heard what he thought was, "Get Rudolph."

Charlie paused.

He hadn't thought about it until now—he had seen all of Santa's reindeer—but he hadn't seen the most famous reindeer of all.

That was when he heard it.

A deep rumble sounded from the darkness, and Charlie slowly turned his head. It started as a snarl, then morphed into a series of barks and growls, and a gnashing of teeth. The sound resonated off the walls and seemed to attack Charlie from all angles. He wasn't sure which way it was coming from. Charlie stood paralyzed, his legs shaking, his heart trapped in his throat.

Charlie's hands dug into the rock, little granules biting his skin. Behind him, he heard a dove in its cage flapping its wings violently, as if sensing the danger. The rabid sounds grew louder, echoing down the tunnel. He pressed himself even flatter against the wall, his lungs cinching tight.

A faint red glow hovered at the far end of the shaft.

Charlie's face slackened. The red glow was *moving*.

The elves' voices heightened. The red glow in front of Charlie grew brighter. The growls lowered as a creature came into view.

A massive, four-legged beast emerged, a cross between a grizzly bear and a dire wolf. It was illuminated by its glowing, red nose, not only lighting the entire mine shaft, but lighting up its huge rack of antlers and its deadly set of teeth that stuck out from its black, hairy lips.

Charlie stumbled backward, eyes blinking, pulse racing, thinking he would never laugh and call *that* creature names.

The ten elves emerged behind Rudolph, holding him by a chained leash. The beast pulled on the leash, yanking, snarling. Drool drizzled from its mouth.

"I told you you wouldn't get far," the elf from earlier said. He eyes flickered red, and his pointy teeth flashed.

The elves laughed, and Rudolph yanked the chain again. The elves tugged the beast back, the tendons in their frail arms straining.

Rudolph stalked forward, keeping his gaze fixed on Charlie.

Charlie edged backward toward the tunnel opening, and his back bumped into a sharp outcropping. A tiny crevice opened up to his right. His heart leapt as he stared into the dark alcove. Making a decision, he jumped inside—just as Rudolph sprung forward—and Charlie squeezed himself into the tiny nook, sucking his stomach in tight.

The beast barked, darting his head around, turning his red nose back and forth, sniffing, searching. His nose illuminated the walls. He paused at the opening of the forbidden tunnel, then slowly rotated its massive head toward Charlie's position.

The red glow casted a shadow from the nook Charlie was in, giving him a moment of obscurity. The beast couldn't see him. For how long, Charlie didn't know. He pulled in a breath, waiting. Then, a deep guttural growl emitted from Rudolph's chest.

This is it, Charlie thought. *This is how it ends.*

Charlie shut his eyes, awaiting his fate.

The beast barked again and snapped its jaws violently, and the elves shouted. The dove's cage hung outside the opening, and Rudolph leapt for the bird, gnashing its teeth. The elves jerked back on the chain.

"Down boy, down!" the elves yelled together.

They finally pulled Rudolph back, and he snarled.

"The boy must've escaped into the main mine," an elf said. "We need to search every inch of this place. The others will be back soon."

The red glow faded as they disappeared from sight.

Charlie couldn't move. He couldn't breathe until he was certain Rudolph was a good distance away. Finally, he crumpled against the nook wall. He gathered himself, knowing he couldn't continue down the main tunnels. He'd have to find another way to get to his teammates.

Charlie straightened, and his eyebrows flew upward.

The elevator.

No one would be guarding it now.

Charlie squeezed out of the crevice and started to sprint out of the forbidden tunnel. The ground gave out from underneath him. His body slipped through the earth, darkness swallowing him whole.

156

17.

I'm reelin' like a merry-go-round...

Charlie hit hard.

His shoulder slammed onto solid ground. He covered his head as dirt and rocks cascaded from above, before a large support beam overhead groaned, and came crashing down. He quickly rolled out of the way, ignoring the pain in his right shoulder.

Charlie held frozen, his body curled up in a ball, his hands wrapped around his head. The debris settled, and the dust cleared. He slowly unfolded.

The large beam laid at an angle from the ground all the way back up into the mining level. Charlie scrambled to his feet. He was lucky to be alive. He'd hoped that all of the noise he'd caused hadn't attracted Rudolph and the elves.

Charlie blinked, and rubbed his eyes. He lifted his hands in front of his face and wiggled his fingers. In all the commotion, he hadn't realized...

He could see.

He didn't have on a mining helmet, and *he could see.*

A sudden whoosh of heat blasted behind him, and the wall in front of him lit up a yellow-orange. His shadow flashed on the rocks, and Charlie spun around.

Where was he?

Charlie stepped forward, and another swoosh of heat hit. Flames exploded beyond a group of rocks in the distance, lighting Charlie's location further. Loose pebbles tumbled beneath Charlie's toes, and he gasped, peeking down. The rocks fell silently into a black chasm. He was on the edge of a cliff.

Charlie's heart reacted, and his breaths came in short, quick bursts. He closed his eyes and swallowed hard.

A low rumble raced above his head. Charlie glanced up, and the rumble grew louder. Over and up, a rail track was suspended in mid-air by large beams. A mine cart roared past on the tracks and curved left around a corner of the precipice on which Charlie stood.

Whoosh. Heat.

Charlie suddenly needed to know where that cart went. He needed to know where the heat and flames were coming from. He needed to get around that corner. Perhaps it led to an exit.

To his left, a narrow ledge followed the corner. One side was a flat, rocky wall, and the other was nothing but the deadly chasm. He eyed the ten-inch ledge and shivered.

He couldn't do this.

Charlie thought of the times Emily would walk along the top edge of the couch, pretending to be a gymnast.

"Charlie! Come play with me!" she would say. "I'm on a balance beam!"

For once in his life, he wished he'd just played along with his little sister.

But what choice did he have? Go back to Rudolph and the elves?

He shook his head and scooted forward, tentatively placing one foot on the narrow ledge. He kept his eyes upward, and his weight as far into the wall as he could. His whole body shook, his stomach quivering. His knees wobbled as he placed his right foot next to his left. He tried to pretend he was Emily, at home on their couch in the safety of their living room, instead of one slip from his death.

Another mine cart rushed by overhead. Dust rained down onto Charlie's head. He pressed himself against the wall, shaking, waiting, until it was safe again.

The cart disappeared around the corner.

Whoosh. Heat.

In the distance, Charlie soft pings reverberated back to him. He wondered if the sounds were the mining kids from above, but the banging didn't appear to be coming from overhead.

The clangs grew louder the further Charlie traveled. A piercing scream rebounded, and Charlie stiffened. Charlie's feet tottered, but he regained his footing, and picked up the pace.

He rounded the corner, and the ledge widened.

Charlie stepped to safer ground and his whole body exhaled.

The track overhead disappeared into a tunnel, and he clambered inside. On his hands and knees, he felt his way through the dark, until he reached the other end.

The scene before him exploded to life.

Larger than the Grand Canyon, the cavern opened up.

Whoosh. Heat.

Elevated rail track curved around the mountainside from every direction, suspended from the ceiling and supported by long stilts—teetering above the dark abyss below. The track twisted and turned, weaved in and out of dark caverns and caves, splitting off into different directions like a roller coaster.

Charlie hated roller coasters.

Another cart passed overhead, and he watched as it curved around the track, where it hurtled toward a gigantic furnace. Flames roared inside the furnace's iron belly, the fire licking up and out from the massive machine. The cart's momentum hit the end of the track, spilling its contents into the fiery opening. The cart rolled back, down another track, and spiraled its way down to Charlie's right, where a conveyor lifted it back up to the top of the tracks to start its journey all over again.

A rattle and a large clunk boomed to the left. Charlie jerked around and watched as coal spilled from a chute that protruded from a wall next to the furnace. The coal fell into the flames causing them to flare out with a WHOOSH. A rush of hot air hit Charlie's face. Charlie's head shot up to the ceiling, and his eyes widened. The coal must have come from above, which could only mean…

This was the Permanent Naughty List.

Whoosh. Heat.

Charlie swayed on his feet.

The flames. The heat. The stifling air. The danger. This place was worse than he imagined. Charlie winced, thinking the mine above him was bad—but this one was worse. This was forever.

Henry. Where was Henry? And the other kids?

Charlie spun around, searching.

That's when he saw him.

Above, and to his left, was little Henry, with a steel collar around his neck, connected to a series of chains looped down around his wrists and ankles. Several elves pushed and pulled Henry over to the edge of the cliff.

He had a harness strapped around his body, which was connected to a line that stretched out over the open pit below. Two elves turned a crank, and a series of ropes and pulleys that carried Henry out over the edge. Charlie tensed, eyes glued. Sweat trickled down his face and neck, but he couldn't move to wipe it off.

The elves continued to turn the crank, and Henry continued outward until he reached his destination.

Charlie finally ripped his gaze away. Hundreds of huge stalactites jutted down from the ceiling. They reminded him of the icicles that hung outside his window at home. He knew they were stalactites and not stalagmites, because of a saying that Emily had taught him:

Stalactites hold tight to the ceiling. Charlie was convinced Emily had always been smarter than him, even at the age of six.

Above him, Henry had pulled out his axe and started hammering at the stalactite. He carefully chipped away the outer surface, until he reached the inside. Within the spike, there were spots that glowed a dimmed orange-red, pulsing from the center. Charlie had never seen anything like it.

Henry pulled out the chunk of glowing rock and placed it in a pouch around his waist. The elves turned the crank in the opposite direction, and Henry slowly drifted back safely onto the cliff.

"Gimme!" One elf hastily grabbed the red glowing rock from Henry's pouch and rushed it over to a cart full of similar rocks. He released the break on the cart, and off it went.

The cart traveled down the track and over his head. It reached the furnace and dumped its load. When the gem-like rocks were sufficiently melted, the large vat tipped, pouring its contents out like a waterfall, the fiery liquid cascading down into a trough where its molten contents traveled to another furnace below.

The orange-red lava, now ribboned with a line of black, exited the furnace and traveled down another trough and into a machine. At the other end of the machine, small drops of the glowing syrup-like substance oozed out of a nozzle and filled tiny glass vials.

Charlie's mouth fell open.

He couldn't believe it took *all* of that work and *all* of that rock just to make the tiny amount liquid. Charlie recognized it as the same liquid that gave Santa's sleigh and his reindeer the ability to fly. An elf snatched a vial and carefully loaded it into a small crate. He gave the crate to another elf who entered the elevator and up he went.

The elevator.

Charlie squinted across the chasm. There was no way he could get to it from here.

Charlie took in the rest of the ginormous space. He wondered where the rest of the kids were. Where Timmy was. Charlie tentatively peeked past the cliff and into the blackness below, trying not to think the worst.

A half dozen elves dragged Henry to another rope and pulley. Some elves pushed, some elves pulled, and some elves tried to nibble on Henry's toes. They leapt and chortled, and Henry tried to kick them off, but there were too many of them.

This wasn't fair. Henry shouldn't be treated like this.

The elves continued to torture him. Laughing. Poking. Prodding.

Henry hadn't done anything wrong. This was Charlie's fault. All of it.

The elves danced around him, shoving Henry toward another cliff.

Charlie's chest squeezed tight. He couldn't watch this. Charlie stepped forward, his fists pumping.

"Leave him alone!" Charlie yelled.

A few elves turned, their ears pricked, their heads popping up over the large ravine. More elves popped up. Their wrinkled faces with their sharp, yellow teeth appeared between the rocks and the crevices.

Henry peeked over his shoulder, the large gap between his teeth visible as his jaw fell open. He shook his head, motioning Charlie to get away.

More elves emerged from their hiding places. Charlie shuffled back, just now realizing what he'd done. He'd only seen a few elves. He didn't realize there were so many. Charlie swallowed.

Whoosh. Heat.

The elves pounced. They sprung from rock to rock, scrambling over the spikes toward Charlie with ease. Charlie did the only thing he could do.

He ran.

Charlie sprinted back into the tunnel, then down towards the ledge. He jumped onto the ridge, this time edging across it as quickly as possible. He didn't even falter.

Light from the flames lit Charlie's path. He leapt over the final bits of the ledge and his shadow fell across the angled, fallen beam. He fumbled up onto the splintered wood and shimmied his way up back into the coal mine.

Charlie pushed past the DANGER and KEEP OUT signs, and back into the mine shaft, not caring where Rudolph was.

He had to get out.

Charlie bolted down the tunnel, back toward the elevator. Behind him, loud barks and roars pierced his ears.

No.

Maybe he *did* care where Rudolph was.

A red glow shone in the distance. The light grew close and fast— illuminating the path ahead of him. Hot breath hit his back, and spittle slapped his cheek. Charlie yelled, and pushed his legs harder. Charlie knew the elves could appear at any moment, but it was better than being eaten alive by this beast.

The elevator came into view, and Charlie's heart thumped faster.

Rudolph's chains clanked, dragging five elves behind, their teeth jarring and their heads bobbing, too dumb to let go.

Charlie eyed the elevator. He wasn't going to make it.

It was too far, and he was slowing down.

His lungs burned and his legs ached.

Voices from down the tunnel started to stir, and more elves came rushing from the mine, their silhouettes red from Rudolph's nose.

Charlie's eyes slid to the right.

The conveyer belt churned, rolling upward, moving at a fast pace.

Charlie glanced back to the elevator.

Making a split-second decision, Charlie turned and leapt onto the conveyer belt, just as Rudolph lunged. The beast missed, skidding into the wall with a thunderous crash. The conveyer swept Charlie upward, drawing Charlie inward, but Rudolph was already back on his feet. The beast jumped onto the belt after him, and snagged the bottom of Charlie's pant leg, dragging him back down.

"No!" Charlie yelled. "Get off!"

Charlie kicked his legs, trying to fend off the beast, but Rudolph's eyes brightened as he growled and hissed, salivating as he towed Charlie closer to his mouth. The elves at the bottom of the conveyor cheered Rudolph on.

Charlie continued to thrash, then spotted the part of the conveyor that went downward, the half that led to the fiery furnace below. Charlie gasped, scrambling away from the downward channel. Rudolph's eyes twinkled, as he hauled Charlie toward the descending duct—knowing it was his certain death.

"I said, let me go!" Charlie thrashed again.

Charlie reared his free foot and kicked. Hard. His foot smacked the beast directly in the glowing nose, and Rudolph yelped, pulling back. Charlie's pajamas ripped, and the beast popped back out of the opening, slamming into the elves like bowling pins.

The conveyer belt whisked Charlie upward, as he disappeared behind the rocky outcropping, leaving Rudolph and the elves behind.

18.

Later on we'll conspire…

Charlie fell with a clonk.

The conveyer belt had carried him up through the mountain and dumped him into Santa's warehouse, onto a massive pile of coal. The black rocks scraped his skin, sending pain along his arms and legs, and under the bottom of his chin. Multiple piles of coal scattered the floor, and a cart full sat off to one side.

Voices sounded down the hall, and Charlie knew he didn't have long. His eyes shot around the space. There was no other exit, save for Santa's door at the far end of the room, but he wouldn't make it there in time. His only hope was to hide.

Charlie started for the cart, thinking it would be the easiest to bury himself in, but then darted for the pile on the right instead. He found a hole at the bottom of the large pile, and wiggled his way in. A few rocks clattered to the cement floor as he buried himself inside.

The door burst open, and footsteps slowly entered.

Charlie peeked through the stack of rocks, a tiny crevice that didn't reveal his location—but showed him just enough to see the scene before him. Rudolph prowled into the room, followed by four elves, all covered in cuts and bruises.

Under the fluorescent light, Rudolph was worse than Charlie imagined. Sagging eyelids with veins that popped out and hung over his face, drool that had crusted in patches over his matted fur, with bald spots that revealed old scars from previous battles. Charlie shook at the thought of how he'd gotten them. Rudolph slunk down, his sharp teeth sticking out from under his red nose, with razor-sharp claws that scraped at the floor with each step.

Rudolph went straight for the cart full of coal and began sniffing.

"Smart," an elf said. "If I were a boy, that'd be the first place I'd hide."

Rudolph easily tipped the cart over with his massive snout. Black rocks scattered everywhere, but the Charlie wasn't there. His pulse spiked, and he tightened his lips against one another, trying to slow his breathing.

The elves split up, and began raking through the piles of coal, sifting through the heavy rocks, throwing them on the ground one by one. He flinched each time a piece hit the warehouse floor and echoed through the room.

"Come on out, Charlie," one elf taunted. "We know you're in here."

"Rudolph's hungry," another said. "We've starved him just for you."

Charlie sat curled up in a ball, his chin to his knees. It was only a matter of time.

The coal continued to clunk. Piece by piece, hitting the floor.

Charlie waited, listening, heart pounding.

Rudolph growled, creeping towards Charlie's stack of coal. He sniffed along the edges, and circled the pile, a red light flashing near the crevice where Charlie's head hid. Charlie drew his knees tighter to his chest. Rudolph's growling deepened.

"Welcome!" a heavy voice said. "Welcome to the place where magic happens!"

Rudolph sidled backwards and the elves halted their search. Charlie released a sigh.

Charlie peered back through the crevice. Santa and Blitzen strode into the room, Santa carrying a burlap sack. He dumped the sack onto the floor and untied the rope at the top. A small girl tumbled out, and Charlie gasped. He covered his mouth again, leaning forward.

"So nice of you to join us, dear," Santa said. "And all thanks to your brother, Charlie. He traded his freedom for yours, you know. It's a shame, isn't it? But it's okay. You'll like it here. Blitzen, tell Emily how much she'll love working here in the mines."

Blitzen's face darkened as his lips twisted up into a smile. "You're going to love it here."

Emily scrambled onto her knees. Her eyes widened as she glanced around the room. The four elves emerged from behind a pile of coal. One elf approached Santa, wringing his filthy hat in his hands.

"Um, Mr. Santa Claus, sir?" The elf gulped, sweat forming on his brow. "A word?"

Santa's soiled eyebrows drew together, his face tightening into a scowl. He bent his large body down to the elf's eye level. "What."

"There's a situation," the elf said, voice low and shaky. "The boy… is missing."

The elf continued to whisper in Santa's ear, and Charlie turned his head slightly, straining to hear.

Heat flushed Santa's face, and his scowl deepened. When the elf finished, Santa's head swung back up, his horns made a large swoosh, and his heavy boots marched forward, his eyes cold and black. Santa gripped Emily by the elbow and yanked her to feet.

"I want to tell you a bed time story, Emily," Santa's voice boomed loud enough as if he somehow knew Charlie could hear him. "Once upon a time, there was a naughty boy who had a sister, and this sister was going to work in the coal mines. But because of this boy's naughtiness, his sister was now going to be put on the Permanent Naughty List, and work in the underground mines forever!"

Charlie's heart dropped. No. Not there. He had seen what it was like to work down there. He thought of poor Henry and the torment he'd endured. He couldn't bear the thought of anyone having to work in those conditions, especially Emily. And she was only five.

Santa tightened his grip and dragged Emily toward the door. Emily's face paled, her blonde curls bouncing on the way. Charlie noticed a crumpled piece of paper in her hand.

"Continue your search for the boy. I'll take her myself," Santa barked to the others. "Since you all are clearly incapable."

Emily dug her feet into the ground and wrenched her arm out of Santa's grasp. Santa looked down at her arm, then glanced up at her face, his brows lifted in surprise.

"You're wrong about Charlie," Emily said. "He isn't naughty. He's a good boy, and a good brother. And he wouldn't do this to me. He wouldn't do what you said he did. He wouldn't!"

Charlie pushed back against the rocks, a lump settling in his throat. He watched Emily plead with Santa, so determined that he was a good person.

"Oh, my dear," Santa said. "You are blind, aren't you?"

Santa seized her elbow once again and started to pull her from the room.

"No! No! Charlie is good! He is!"

Santa dragged her through the doorway.

Emily glanced behind her. Her fingers spread wide and she released the paper in her hands. The paper drifted to the floor.

The elves followed Santa from the room. Rudolph stopped and snarled where Charlie hid again, his breath pungent as it drifted in through the rocks. His black eyes scanned past the coal, and Charlie held his breath.

"Rudolph! Come!" Blitzen commanded.

The beast huffed, but followed. Charlie let out a shaky breath.

Emily's voice drifted from the hallway, still defending Charlie, still yelling at what a good person her brother was, but her voice faded until the elevator descended, down to the Permanent Naughty List.

Charlie itched to climb out, to save her, to storm after them, to grab Emily and make a run for it, but then what? If they were both caught, they'd never make it out of there.

He sat, listening, for what seemed like hours, nothing heard but the churn of the conveyer belt and the soft buzz of the lights overhead. Charlie hid, unable to get Emily's pleading face out of his mind.

Without any sign of the elevator opening again, Charlie carefully worked his way out through the bottom of the pile, careful not to cause the rocks to fall. He raced over to the paper on the floor.

He took one look at the page and slumped onto the nearest stack of coal. It was Emily's drawing he'd scribbled over. He'd assumed she'd just thrown it away, but she hadn't. Why had she kept it? Charlie turned it over. In Emily's neat scrawl, it had a personal message to Santa on the back:

Dear Santa,

Please forgive my brother, Charlie. He really is a nice brother. He is not as naughty as you might think.

If it helps, I will give up my presents so that Charlie may get
some.

Love,

Emily Peters.

Charlie sat back on the pile, his whole body slumping. Tears pricked his eyes, and his head ached. Emily had just wanted her big brother to love her, but he'd had a cold heart. Since birth, Charlie had done nothing but torture her and tease her, done anything to get what he wanted, even if it meant throwing her under the bus, just like he'd done to her here and now. He remembered all the times where he could have been a good brother—where he could have played with her or helped her or talked with her or showed her that he cared. She was so nice to him, and he had been horrible to her.

Emily didn't deserve this. She was the good one—the one who only wanted good things for other people. No, she didn't deserve this at all. He did.

What had he done? What could he do?

Charlie placed his hands over his face and scrubbed. He groaned and shook his head. There was nothing he could do. He was alone and it was too late. It seemed the only way in or out of this place was the

176

sleigh.

An idea crackled in the back of his mind.

He lowered his hands.

The sleigh.

Charlie thought back to how the elf called out "The North Pole" when they first brought him here. That was how the sleigh traveled from place to place—you had to call out the destination. Charlie glanced back at the picture in his hand, then glanced over to the small, circular table to where the Naughty and Nice List had been earlier.

Charlie jumped up from where he sat.

He had a plan.

19.

From now on our troubles will be miles away...

Charlie glanced over his shoulder as he rushed to the middle of the room.

The Naughty and Nice book sat on the small table, standing out in the drab warehouse like the brightest star on the top of a Christmas tree. Charlie snatched the quill off the table and opened the book, furiously setting to work, all the while, keeping his ears open and alert.

With his work complete, Charlie shut the book, ready for the next phase of his plan.

He headed over to the long table that was littered with odds and ends. Finding what he needed, Charlie turned and stared down the warehouse door. He knew beyond the door was the elevator. It was the only conventional way down to the mine—but it was far too risky. He'd have to go back down the way he came—the conveyer belt.

Charlie tiptoed across the room and hefted himself up onto the end of the conveyor, avoiding incoming rocks. He placed his hands on the edge of the metal railing and crawled inside the machine. Even though the belt moved in the opposite direction than he wanted to go, Charlie recalled the multiple times he went down the "up" escalator at the mall, embarrassing his parents. He smiled at the memory, knowing he could do this.

The belt churned, and he pushed his feet downward. He made his way to the split in the belt, and leapt up, straddling the belt, with his feet and hands wedged into the mountain wall for support. He settled himself on a small ledge, in a stable position, watching the coal go up into Santa's workshop, and the coal go down into the Permanent Naughty List below. He waited for nightfall, hoping no one would discover his hideout.

He sat for what felt like hours, his legs shaking from the awkward position. An itch bristled the middle of his back, and he'd do anything to scratch it. His stomach rumbled. He found himself craving his favorite food—a grilled cheese sandwich with grape jelly on top— heck, even thoughts of gingerbread made his mouth water. He swore he would never complain about food again.

Finally, the conveyor slowed until it came to a screeching halt.

The sudden quiet made Charlie's ears pop. The belt's constant hum still echoed in his head.

Charlie listened as the miners marched to their sleeping quarters, and he calculated the time for the elves and the reindeer to take their posts—for the moment he could continue his plan.

Footsteps sounded.

Hooves clopped.

Bells jingled.

One. Two. Three. Charlie counted, bracing himself. He jumped down from his hiding spot, slid off of the conveyor, and landed onto the dirty mine floor with a thud.

Two reindeer patrolled off to the right, antlers tall, eyes scanning the area. Charlie scrambled back away from them, into the shadows of the tunnel wall. He held frozen, eyes wide, hoping they hadn't seen him.

The reindeer passed, disappearing into the elevator up and out of sight. Charlie worked his way over to the single, dying torch hanging on the wall. He retrieved the flame, not enough light to expose him from afar, but just light enough so that he could see where he was going. He headed down the sleeping hall.

His feet were quiet on the muddy ground and, despite the pain, this time he was glad he didn't have his slippers—the clay felt cool on his feet.

In the distance, he heard faint sounds of pick axes hitting rock. Someone must have been sentenced to work after bedtime. Charlie's heart squeezed as he imagined his little sister dangling in midair over that deep, dark chasm, chipping away at the stalactites. She'd be so scared, hungry, and tired, wondering if her brother would ever come to her rescue. He took a deep, shuddering breath. He had to continue onward.

When Charlie approached his sleeping quarters, he paused outside the entrance, wondering if he was doing the right thing. This decision could ruin everything. But when he heard Rose moan as Zach let out a huge fart, a smile lifted on Charlie's face, and he knew he'd made the right choice.

Charlie ducked inside the alcove, bending underneath the low outcropping, and balanced the dying torch against the wall. His foot hit the deadly mattress, and a sharp spring poked his toe. He bit back a cry, swallowing down the pain.

Toe throbbing, he edged back, maneuvering through the other mattresses, until he found Rose. He bent down, the low light highlighting the beauty mark by her right eye. Knowing she would probably scream or knock him out if he shook her awake, Charlie gently pinned her shoulders with one arm to the mattress and covered her mouth with his other hand.

Her eyes flew wide open, the whites almost glowing in the dark. She yelped, the sound muffled, and she shoved Charlie off of her with ease. Charlie fell back, landing hard on his backside. She sat upright, and Charlie raised a finger to his lips.

"Shh," he whispered. "It's me, Charlie."

"I know who it is," she hissed. "What the heck are you doing here?"

He rubbed his hip. "It's good to see you, too."

Rose crossed her arms. "I didn't say it was good to see you."

Zach sat up, groaning. He caught sight of Charlie and immediately sat up.

"Unbelievable," Zach said. "I thought you were sent home. Didn't ruin our lives enough, so you needed to come take our food rations too?"

"No," Charlie said. "You guys, I—"

"We don't want to hear it, Charlie," Rose spat. "We're sick of hearing it."

"Don't worry," Zach said to Rose. "I know how to take out the trash."

Zach stood up and the mattress creaked. Rose also stood, and advanced forward.

"You guys," Charlie said, backing away a bit. "I came back to help you. I know how to get us out of here."

Rose uncrossed her arms. "Oh yeah? And why should we believe you?"

"And why would you help us when you already had an out?" Zach asked.

Charlie paused, and silence stretched between them.

"My... my little sister is here," Charlie said, voice low.

Rose let out a small gasp.

"It's all my fault. I'm not leaving here until I get her out. And I'm not leaving here until I get you out, too. All of you."

Charlie swallowed, then swallowed again. "But..." he hesitated, "I need your help."

Zach clicked his tongue. "You have some nerve. Why should we help you and risk getting put onto the Permanent Naughty List?"

Charlie lifted up his palms, before he slowly lowering them. "Because we're a team."

Rose and Zach looked at one another and rolled their eyes.

"No," Charlie stated, correcting himself. "Because we're a *family*. I know I may not have shown it, but I consider you guys my family. Families look out for one another. Families fight for one another. I'm here to prove it. I want to prove it. For once in my entire life I want to prove it. Please."

"I don't know," Zach said, scratching the back of his head. "What do you think, Rose?"

Her eyes lifted, and her lips curved up to one side. "Family, you say?" She thought for a moment, rubbing her finger across her chin.

"Alright," she finally said. "What's the plan?"

The next morning, the miners lined up in the tunnel with an extra bounce in their step. Whispers passed from line to line, eyes sparkling with excitement. Zach and Rose had spread the word about Charlie's plan, and the miners kept the plan sealed shut, smiles on their faces as they walked past the reindeer guards.

Blitzen stood at the end of the tunnel, handing out the two-rock ration of calcium carbide for the day. The kids marched up, received the rocks, and instead of plopping both rocks into their helmets, they dropped only *one* rock into their lamps and secretly hid the other rock in their palms. Some kids were able to keep a straight face as they passed Blitzen, other kids pressed their lips together, fighting back a smile.

As the kids lit their lamps, filing into the mine shaft, Charlie's hand emerged from the shadows, and each of the kids dropped their hidden rock into his palm. Charlie pocketed the stolen rocks, with a mischievous smile on his face.

It was time to put the rest of his plan into action.

20.

The fire is slowly dying...

Charlie ripped the hem of his pajama pants and tore off the dirty fabric into a square. He placed the collected calcium carbide rocks in the middle and tied the corners of the material into a bundle.

At Zach and Rose's workstation, Charlie took a chunk of coal and rubbed it all over his face and neck, hoping it'd blend him into the surrounding darkness. It matched his already blackened pajamas. Zach and Rose smiled at his cleverness, watching Charlie as he waited.

Halfway through the morning, the miners' helmets started to dim. Comet and Donder marched up and down the mine, investigating the situation. They whispered to each other, faces growing somber, their eyes narrowing at the unexpected wilting lamps. Finally, he heard them whisper, "Charlie."

Blitzen trotted up to the two reindeer, his muscles flexed, his hairy eyebrows stern.

"Get the others!" Blitzen ordered. "How did you let this

happen?"

Comet and Donder glanced at each other, paralyzed.

"I said go!" Blitzen yelled.

The two reindeer raced off.

Blitzen stalked toward Charlie's teammates, and Charlie retreated deeper into the shadows. He crossed his beefy arms, glaring.

"I know you know something," Blitzen said. "What are you two hiding from me?" He stuck his piercing eyes right into Rose's face. "Where is Charlie?"

Rose didn't flinch. She planted her pick axe into the ground and tilted her head to the side. "I don't know what you're talking about.

Blitzen turned on Zach so fast, even Charlie blinked. "And you? Are you going to lie too?"

"Are you kidding?" Zach snapped. "Charlie is a filthy liar. He deceived us all. If I saw him again, I would ruin that kid's life so hard he wouldn't know what hit him."

Blitzen rocked back, studying Zach closely. "You better both be telling the truth. Or you know the consequences. And I can find a worse consequence than the Permanent Naughty List."

Charlie stared at Zach, his heart rocketing. For a moment,

Charlie wondered if Zach was telling the truth. Was Zach just playing along with Charlie so he could turn him in? No, Charlie stopped himself from going down that path again. He trusted Zach, and he trusted Rose.

Lamps from across the mine began to shut off. Blitzen spun around. To the left, more helmets blacked out. Then to the right. The shaft darkened.

Blitzen stomped forward. "Guards!"

He took off, galloping down the middle of the mine.

Charlie moved away from the shadows, grinning. "Thanks, guys. Great job."

"Go!" Rose said, shooing him. "You don't have much time!"

"Yeah. Okay!" Charlie slapped his friends on the back and turned right. "See you guys soon!"

Charlie darted along the rail track, deeper into the mine. He planted his feet right in the middle. No turning back now.

He cupped his hands up to his mouth and yelled, "Did you lame-o reindeer think you could outsmart me?" His voice reverberated down the shaft. "Not a chance! I'm Charlie Peters, and I'm the only kid who's outsmarted Santa, his reindeer, and his elves! You'll never outsmart me! And you'll never catch me!" He waved his arms, and he dashed toward the dining hall.

"Get him!" Charlie heard Dasher yell.

Rudolph snarled and barked, and dozens of footsteps charged down the mine after him. Charlie's mind did summersaults, wondering if his plan would work, wondering if he was a fool for leading the entire reindeer guard after him, but he shook his head and focused. He only had one shot.

The other children passed him, sneaking by on either side of him. Charlie knew where they were headed. He knew the reindeer weren't paying attention to them, since they were all so focused on him. He trusted that Rose and Zach would help them up onto the conveyor where they would be whisked upward toward their freedom. He smiled to himself.

Approaching his planned hiding spot, Charlie ducked into a small alcove inside the tunnel wall. He prayed his dark disguise would work.

Rudolph and the reindeer guards slowed their pace, as they came to the fork in the tunnels.

"Which way?" Cupid asked.

"Rudolph will tell us," Dancer said.

Rudolph growled, lowering his body to all fours, drool oozing from his mouth. His claws dug into the loose dirt in the ground, and he sniffed, the sound a combination between a huff and a snort. He circled the area, moving in and out of the dining, sleeping, and mining tunnels.

Charlie slowly bent down, careful not to move too fast. He picked up a rock he'd left there earlier that morning.

Rudolph sniffed along the walls and crevices. Charlie only had moments before Rudolph's red glowing nose lit up the area, exposing him. Charlie cocked his arm back and hurled the rock into the sleeping hall. It bounced off the interior walls.

Rudolph snapped his head up. He lunged towards the sound, dragging the reindeer guard with him.

Charlie listened as the footsteps trailed away. His heartbeat throbbed on either side of his head. He needed to make a run for it, but he also needed to make sure it was safe. He hoped all the kids had made it out. Waiting a few more heartbeats, Charlie inched out, and then bolted from the alcove, sprinting back toward the conveyer.

In Charlie's peripheral, a shadow darted out next to him. A loud bark resounded, followed by ear splitting gnashing and howling sounds.

"Rudolph's got him!" Charlie heard a reindeer yell.

No!

Footsteps pounded after him, and Charlie pushed his legs faster. He hadn't tricked Rudolph after all. The tunnel ahead was pitch-black, but Charlie knew if he kept his feet along the cool rail tracks, he'd find his way to the conveyer.

Rudolph gained on Charlie. The beast leapt, his claws brushing his back, but Charlie dodged to his right. Rudolph went tumbling, slamming into the tunnel wall, howling. Charlie smirked, and pushed faster. Growling sounded again, and within seconds, Rudolph was back behind him. Charlie's jaw slackened, but he narrowed his eyes. He had a good lead, and he knew he could still make his escape.

Charlie's toe caught on a wooden tie rail, and pain shot up his leg. He toppled over, falling face first. His chin hit hard, and the bundle of rocks flew into the air.

"No!" Charlie yelled.

The bundle landed somewhere in the dark. He crawled on his hands and knees, groping around, patting the dirt, frantically searching for the stack of rocks.

Rudolph's nose shone from behind, casting a dim, red glow. As Rudolph and the guards approached, the light grew brighter and brighter.

Charlie's heart raced faster and faster.

"Where *is* it?" Charlie yelled.

Soft fabric met Charlie's hand and he gripped the bundle, scrambling to his feet. "Yes!"

Charlie eyed his destination. His workstation. He'd spent endless hours mining coal with Zach and Rose there, over and over and over again. Rudolph barked and his teeth gnashed right next to his ear. Charlie cried out and sprinted faster. The guards closed in, but Charlie had just enough of a lead to run up to the area where the ceiling of the mine had started to collapse on Rose the other day.

Charlie's feet splashed through the large, familiar puddle. With the entire reindeer guard behind him, Charlie tossed the bundle over his shoulder. It landed in the puddle, and an immediate reaction from the calcium carbide began.

Charlie grabbed the helmet Zach had been instructed to leave for him. Fumbling with the lamp, he struck the flint. Sparks flew, but no flame.

"No!"

He struck the flint again.

Nothing.

Rudolph and the reindeer closed in.

Charlie's heart thudded.

"Come on," he pleaded. "Light!"

He struck the flint again and a small flame emitted from the lamp.

"Yes!"

Charlie tossed the lit lamp into the puddle and everything went white.

Fire erupted outward, everything detonating into a massive explosion. The ceiling collapsed, huge chunks of rock and coal rained down, completely blocking the mine—sealing the tunnel shut. Charlie had glanced back just in time to see Rudolph's red glow fade away behind the debris. Rudolph whimpered behind the barrier, and the reindeer called for help, but their voices were swallowed up behind the barricade.

Charlie stood staring at the pile of rocks, heart hammering, breaths fast.

It had worked.

Phase one of his plan had worked. Not wanting to find out how long the barrier would keep the reindeer contained, Charlie backed away, ran to the conveyer belt, and hopped on, riding it up to the warehouse.

###

"Charlie!" Rose said, rushing over. She threw her arms around him in a big hug. Her auburn hair looked black with the streaks of coal smudged through the strands. "You made it!"

"Hey, nice work," Zach said, punching him in the shoulder. "I didn't think you could do it. Pretty impressive."

"Thanks," Charlie said, rubbing his shoulder.

Charlie peered around the warehouse. The miners were hovered around the tables full of trinkets, picking up different baubles that caught their eye.

"This is my music box!" one little girl said.

"And my slingshot!" another little boy said.

"And I've been looking for this puzzle piece forever!" another kid said.

The rest of the kids chatted in circles, bodies covered in charcoal, faces stretched wide in wonder.

Charlie stepped deeper into the room.

"Good job, you guys," Charlie choked out, impressed with the teamwork. If they hadn't worked together, they wouldn't have made it this far. "Are you ready to go home?"

The room burst into cheers, and Charlie felt his throat tighten.

"We still have to make it to the sleigh. It could be dangerous. Are you sure you all want to do this?"

Rose clasped Charlie's hand and squeezed. "We're sure."

Charlie nodded and moved to the door. He motioned the kids into the hallway.

One by one, the miners walked through the door, eyes wide at the crystalized bits of rock that reflected off of the buzzing, golden bulbs. Charlie led the group down the hall toward their freedom.

As they exited the hall, the children gasped. Sitting right in front of them was Santa's sleigh. They rushed over to the aged structure, jumping inside, running their hands along the peeling paint and rusted exterior.

Rose started to move forward, but Charlie grabbed her shoulder. She turned.

"Help everyone get aboard," he said. "I need to go find my sister. And I hope…" Charlie took a deep breath. "It shouldn't take long. But if I'm not back in five minutes, you need to go ahead without me, okay?"

Rose's forehead pinched. "Yeah, I don't think so."

"I'm serious, Rose. Look at all these kids. You need to get them out. I already told you how to call out the address and the sleigh will take you there. Please promise me that you'll get these kids home."

Rose searched Charlie's eyes, her thin brows pulling together. Her lips pouted, but finally, she relaxed.

"Fine," she said. "Five minutes. Maybe six. But then we're gone."

"Done."

Charlie took one last look at Zach, Rose, and at the smiling kids getting settled in the sleigh. He stepped inside the elevator and placed his hand on the red lever. He was going down below to the Permanent Naughty List. And no one could stop him.

21

See the blazing yule before us…

The elevator rammed to a stop.

Charlie pulled open the black gate. The heat hit him first. It reminded him of back home, when his mom would retrieve the fish sticks from the oven, and the hot air would hit his face—though that wasn't quite as deadly. Charlie poked his head outside the elevator. He cocked his ears, listening.

Silence.

He cautiously stepped forward.

The dark chasm stretched in front of him like a bottomless pit, and long, wooden beams shot up out of the black, supporting the rail track that crisscrossed overhead. Above the tracks, rows of pointy stalactites hung down, lit by the flames of the massive furnace, giving them an eerie glow that made Charlie feel like he was walking into the mouth of an alligator.

An empty cart zipped past Charlie, and he jumped. His whole

body felt tight—like he was a string ready to be plucked. The cart zoomed to the left, stopping where the conveyer lifted it back up to its starting point. Charlie had no choice but to head right.

He followed on the ledge, alongside the tracks next to the mountain, zigzagging his way upward. His jaw dropped as snuck past the multiple furnaces, troughs, and machines that smelted the raw material into the magical liquid.

He spotted a crate full of empty vials and slid his gaze over to the large machine working next to it. Charlie snatched a vial and placed it under a spout and turned a spigot. Glowing red-orange liquid oozed out into the vial. Charlie corked it, put it into his pocket, and continued forward, his mouth curving up into a smile.

Charlie paused and peered upward, past the blasts of flame and sharp rocks. He remembered Henry was at the top of the mine. If Henry was there, then Emily might be too. But there could be elves—or worse, Santa. He didn't see any elves, but he knew they were hiding.

Narrowing his eyes, he pushed his shoulders back, and continued the climb up the mountain.

Charlie's eyes were wide as he passed furnaces and cascading waves of glowing lava. Sweat stuck to his skin, beading on his forehead and neck. His fingers and toes cramped and ached from gripping the ridge so tight, but he continued onward, keeping his eyes and ears alert.

Finally, he reached the top ledge. He peeked down, and his head spun as he took in the multiple layers of machines and workstations, along with the rail tracks that twisted and turned above the bottomless chasm.

Behind him, rows of prison cells were carved into the side of a rock wall. Kids huddled inside the cells, some gripping the bars, some curled up onto the ground.

Charlie's stomach turned.

Emily.

She had to be here.

Charlie patted his pockets. He wished he'd brought that piece of coiled wire. He glanced around, before a flash caught his eye. To the right, a large iron key hung on a hook next to the cells.

What?

He couldn't believe his luck. He dashed over, snatched the key, and began unlocking the cells.

As the prison doors opened, kids rubbed their eyes and gasped. Some patted Charlie on the back and cheered. Some just opened their mouths, speechless. Charlie unlocked their chains.

"Follow the mountain down to the elevator," Charlie said. "And be careful!"

Two by two, the kids headed down the mountain. He frantically searched for Emily, but no blonde, bouncy curls were in the crowd of dirty kids.

Charlie opened the last cell, and Henry's head popped up behind Timmy's.

"Henry!" Charlie said. "You're here! I'm so happy to see you!"

Henry stumbled back, doing a double take, all the blood draining from his face. His onesie pajamas were all but ripped to shreds.

"What are you doing here?" Timmy asked.

"I'm here to set you free," Charlie whispered.

Charlie turned to Henry and unlocked his chains. Henry's mop of sandy hair hung over his face, his eyes wide as Charlie set him free.

"You need to get to the elevator," Charlie said. "The others have already headed down. Take the elevator up as far up as it will go. The sleigh and the rest of the kids are waiting to take you home." Charlie surveyed the area. "Do you know where my sister is?"

"Is that who that little girl was?" Timmy asked. "We all saw

Santa bring her in, but we don't know where Santa took her."

Charlie threw Henry a pleading glance. Henry looked away.

"Okay. Well, here, take this." Charlie reached into his pocket and handed Henry the vial. "Give this to Rose. She'll know what to do with it."

The two boys started to leave, but Charlie tapped Henry on the shoulder.

"Henry," he said. "It's good to see you. And... watch out for the elves. They could be anywhere. Are you sure you'll be okay?"

A sly smile curled across Henry's face. Inside his shirtsleeve, Henry slid out a broken axe handle. He held it up like a bat.

Charlie took in the makeshift weapon, and then grinned at Henry. "Zach was right," he said. "You are a dude with secrets." Charlie patted Henry on the shoulder. "Now, go!"

The two boys rushed off, and Charlie moved past the cells, toward more stalactites.

Charlie weaved around the mountainside, looking for any sign of Emily. He passed the top of the track, where a few carts sat. After a while, he heard the elevator leave. He let out a long exhale, but his lungs still felt tight. *Where was his sister?*

He rounded one more corner.

There.

A single cell was cut into the mountain, and Charlie saw a small form curled up inside.

He stopped.

Blonde hair. Nightgown. Bouncy curls.

Charlie's heart swelled, and tears burned behind his eyes. A relieved smile stretched over his face.

"Emily!"

Charlie raced over and stuck the key into the lock. The lock clicked, and Emily lifted her head. Her face lit up and she jumped to her feet.

"Charlie"

Charlie swung the gate open, and Emily ran to him, throwing her tiny arms tight around his waist.

"I knew you wouldn't leave me here," she said. "I knew you'd come for me. I knew you were good."

Charlie glanced down at her blonde head, and something in him softened. He didn't see her as a pest or a target, but as his little sister. He blinked, and more tears stung his eyes. He saw himself in a new light, too. He saw himself as a big brother, and that he would do anything to protect her.

"Come on," Charlie said, brushing the hair from her face. "Let's get you home."

Charlie unlocked her chains, and he winced, looking at the raw marks on her wrists and ankles.

As they exited the cell, a sick feeling stirred in his gut. This was too easy. There were no elves. The key just happened to be there. All the kids getting out. It all started to feel like he was being set up.

They moved back past the cells and stopped.

Emily gasped.

Before them, blocking the path down the mountainside, were eight elves—but not just any elves—the original eight elves who had taken Charlie from his home that night on Christmas Eve. Charlie imagined they were seeking revenge for outsmarting them. The elves lifted their fingernails and smiled their pointy-toothed smiles.

Emily screamed.

Charlie grabbed his sister's arm. "Run!"

The elves gave chase.

Charlie led Emily to the carts he'd seen earlier. The first one was filled to the max. Charlie pulled the brake release, and it rolled backwards, racing down the track.

The elves gained speed, and Charlie hurried to the second cart. It was only partially full. Emily and Charlie hopped in. The elves reached the cart just as Charlie released the break. It rolled down the track, leaving the elves behind.

Six elves boarded carts of their own—three elves in one cart, three elves in the other. One cart went down the same track, following Charlie and Emily, but the other cart pulled a track switch lever, and they branched off to a different track. The other two elves scurried on foot down the mountainside.

Charlie and Emily whipped around the track. It bobbed up and down, the long stilts making the track sway. Wind whipped in their faces, and the elves on the track behind them gained. Charlie figured it was because they were lighter, giving them more speed.

"Move to the front of the cart!" Charlie yelled to Emily.

Emily's face was wide with terror, but she obeyed.

They picked up a little speed, and Charlie faced forward, gripping onto the wooden cart tight.

Air stung his eyes, and he tried not to look down. The track twisted up, down, and around, weaving in and out of caves and caverns. He wanted to wretch, but had no time for that.

In his peripheral vision, a cart pulled up alongside them, running parallel to their track. The elves cackled and licked their lips.

Emily seized Charlie around the middle and buried her head into his back. "Don't let them get us, Charlie!"

A bump smashed into them from behind, and Charlie felt himself thrown forward.

Emily screamed again.

The other cart had caught up. One of the elves dove out towards them. The elf's nails scraped Emily's back, but he missed her, and disappeared behind the cart.

Wind whistled in Charlie's ears. "Where'd he go!?"

Charlie glanced over his shoulder. The cart took a sharp turn, and the elf popped up, his fingers clinging to the back of the cart, pulling himself inside.

"Let me nibble your toes!" he said, voice hoarse, grinning.

"Emily! Get back!" Charlie yelled, pushing her behind him.

Emily scrambled backwards and the elf hopped inside. Charlie recognized the elf's crooked nose.

The elf crept forward, laughing, the wind blowing his thinning hair. "I'll start with the baby toe and work my way to the big one."

Charlie clasped the sides of the cart and brought both knees to his chest. He punched his legs out—and for the second time that week— kicked him square in the nose. The elf howled and flew out of the cart into the dark ravine.

"My nose!" his voice echoed.

Charlie dusted off his hands, smiling, until Emily shrieked.

He whipped around.

Three elves were pulling Emily from the cart.

Charlie leapt forward and grabbed onto her feet. From one track to the other, her limbs were stretched from cart to cart, her body in a tug of war. The elves heaved. And Charlie hauled.

Emily's face scrunched tight. "Charlie! Help!"

Charlie tugged, but it was three against one. His fingers cramped, and they were slipping. He glimpsed up ahead. The tracks were about to turn in opposite directions.

"Charlie, please!"

The elves smiled, then yanked.

Emily bit down hard on one of the elf's knuckles. The elf yelped and let go.

Charlie tugged again, and the momentum drove Emily backwards, freeing Emily from their grip. They fell back into their cart, just as the cart took a sharp left. The three elves also fell back, causing their cart to tip sideways on two wheels. The cart shot off the tracks and sailed downward into the darkness.

Charlie watched as they disappeared.

"Charlie, look!" Emily shouted, pointing straight ahead.

The two elves on foot stood on the ledge ahead of them, both grinning as they approached. One swung a chain over his head, with a hook connected to the end. The other elf rubbed his hands together, chuckling.

Charlie searched the cart. He rifled through the rocks and picked up a good-sized stone.

He took aim and chucked it at the elf. The rock met its target square in the forehead. Dazed, the elf fell over the side of the cliff. The chain and hook went flying, ricocheting off the coal chute above their heads, causing it to come loose from its mooring. An avalanche of coal spilled out, burying the other elf.

"Nooooo!" the elf yelled, voice muffled.

Charlie and Emily ducked as the hook and chain landed in their cart, just missing them by inches.

Their cart swung around another bend, wind brushing their faces, the bumpy track jarring their teeth, before a wave of hot air hit.

The huge furnace came into view, its flames belching out at the sides. The cart full of mined rocks Charlie had released at the top of the mountain raced just ahead. Charlie watched as it hit the bumper at the end of the track, and sent its contents into the furnace opening, a puff of smoke and flame spilling out.

Charlie gripped Emily's arm. "Emily… don't look…"

She blinked at him blankly, until she noticed the furnace. Her face went white.

"Don't worry!" Charlie yelled. "There's got to be something—" Charlie took in his surroundings, his gaze darting everywhere. In the cart. The rocks. At the machinery. On the track.

The track.

There was a track switcher—just like the one the elves had used above.

Charlie picked up a rock, its surface cold and rough, the jagged edges digging into his palms. He gripped the object, slick in his hands.

"Emily, duck!" he yelled.

Emily obeyed, and Charlie reached back and threw.

The rock sailed into the air and missed the switch by a mile.

Hot air flew into their faces as the cart sped faster toward the furnace. Charlie gripped another rock. Emily whimpered. Charlie reached back and threw again. It whizzed past its target.

"Charlie!" Emily pointed behind them. The other cart full of elves followed closely behind, their arms waving, their eyes wide with worry as they pointed to the furnace.

"Don't worry about them!" Charlie shouted. "I've got this!"

Emily ducked back down and covered her head. Charlie picked up another rock and wiped it on his shirt.

"Come on," he whispered. He tightened the rock in his hand and pulled in a deep breath. Zooming in on the switch, he drew back his arm, and hurled the rock a third time.

Bingo.

The rock connected with the switch, hitting it dead on. The track ahead shifted, and their cart careened right.

"You did it!" Emily threw her arms around Charlie.

The elves behind them hooped and hollered, their fists pumping in the air, before they lowered their arms and leaned forward. Their faces tightened again, and their eyes flashed red, glaring.

"They're still after us!" Emily cried.

The cart took another dip, and they whooshed around another corner. Charlie's stomach flew up into his mouth.

Charlie glanced up as a large vat of molten lava tipped, dumping its red-orange contents down in waterfalls into troughs below. Several carts traveled behind the cascading magma. Drops of the scalding hot liquid landed onto the carts' railings, burning holes through the metal edges.

Charlie lifted his brows. He eyed the chain and hook that had been dropped into the cart earlier.

He had an idea.

Their cart traveled down and passed underneath a trough, and Charlie picked up the chain. He analyzed the distance between him and the support beam next to the trough. Timing it just right, he swung the chain and hook, sending the hook flying. It wrapped itself around one of the support beams, and he braced his feet against the back of the cart as the chain pulled tight. Charlie used every bit of strength he had to keep hold of the chain. The beam broke, and the trough ripped free, tipping, sending its hot contents down onto the track behind them.

The track hissed and sizzled, and the wood and metal dissolved before Charlie's eyes.

The elves' wicked smiles disappeared, their faces open with shock. Their cart dropped, falling off into the chasm below.

Emily covered her mouth.

Charlie sat back.

Their cart took one last turn, and it bumped to a stop, reaching the bottom of the track.

"Come on," Charlie said. He hoisted Emily out of the cart and onto solid ground. He turned and hefted himself out, too, hitting the ground, rolling. When he came to a stop, he brushed off his hands and sat up.

"I can't believe we survived," Charlie said. "Right?"

Emily didn't answer.

Charlie jumped to his feet and glanced around.

"Emily?"

Nothing but the sound of rushing lava answered him.

"Emily! Where are you?"

He scanned the hanging stalactites and at the empty cave before him. His heart plummeted.

A deep chuckle resonated, ricocheting off the surrounding walls. "Looking for her?"

Charlie spun around. "Emily!"

Santa Claus emerged from the shadows, standing tall and firm, one hand holding Emily by the elbow in a solid grip.

Charlie tightened his fists.

"Let her go!" Charlie demanded. "She hasn't done anything wrong!"

"Oh, no no no. She hasn't done anything wrong. No, she's a good little girl." Santa stroked the top of her head. "But if you want her, my boy, you... will have to come... and get her." He smiled, and his rotted teeth looked red in the dim light.

Charlie took a step forward, but hesitated.

A scowl came across Emily's face. "I might be a good little girl, but you are a bad bad man!"

She reared her foot back and kicked Santa in the shin. He shouted, releasing his grip. Charlie darted in and grabbed his sister. They bolted toward the elevator.

"No!" Santa boomed.

His heavy boots pounded after them.

Charlie reached the elevator, but the car wasn't there. They didn't have time to wait for it.

"Charlie! What are we going to do?" Emily cried.

Santa's boots pounded faster.

Charlie tightened his grip on Emily's hand. "To the ledge!"

"What?"

"Run!"

They took off, beelining it for the cliff, toward the deadly ledge. Santa followed. They didn't slow their pace.

"Charlie...?" Emily asked. "What are we doing?"

Hot air breezed into their faces, and Charlie gave Emily a sidelong glance. "Do you trust me?" Charlie asked.

"Of course I do," she responded without hesitation.

An empty cart wheeled past. Charlie measured the distance between Emily and the cart.

Santa picked up his pace and bounded after them, the ground shaking with every step. They were keeping pace with the cart, but Santa was gaining fast. Not too long now.

Charlie reached into his pocket and pulled out the leather bag of marbles that he had taken from Santa's warehouse.

Santa's feet boomed closer.

Charlie loosened the bag's string.

Feet drummed faster.

He dumped the bag over.

More pounding.

Marbles released.

"See the cart?" Charlie yelled. "Jump!" The two of them leapt into the mine car.

The small glass balls rolled, skipping and hopping along the ground, catching underneath Santa's large boots. Santa slipped on the marbles, his feet flying up and out from underneath him. He hit the ground with a thunderous crash. He rolled out of control, his momentum carrying him across the ground and over the edge of the cliff.

Charlie looked over the side of the cart just in time to see Santa's shocked face fade into the darkness below.

Charlie gripped his sister into a hug. "It's okay, Emily. We're going to be fine."

The mine cart connected with the conveyor and carried Charlie and Emily back up to the top of the mine. They'd have to make one more trip down, but this time, they'd walk.

Charlie still hated roller coasters.

22.

I'll be home for Christmas…

Charlie and Emily whizzed upward.

Emily kept her arms wrapped around Charlie as the elevator ascended. Charlie couldn't take his eyes off of her. He was so relieved she was okay. She peeked up at him and smiled. He forced a smile back, but his eyes darted away. It'd been longer than five minutes. He'd instructed Rose to leave. He was sure she and the others were gone. They'd find another way out. They had to.

The elevator came to a stop, and the gate opened.

"Charlie, look!" Emily's finger flew outward.

Charlie lifted his head, and his heart stopped.

No.

Unbelievable.

Rose leaned against the sleigh, her arms crossed, and a smile on her face.

"You really thought I was just going to leave without you?" she asked. "Family's don't abandon each other."

Emily rushed over and threw her arms around Rose. "I don't know who you are," she said. "But you're my new best friend."

Rose pulled out of the hug and lifted her brows at Charlie. She flipped her hair over her shoulder and held up the vial of magic liquid. "Ready to go home?"

Charlie looked over the sleigh. Kids took up every inch of space, some sitting on laps, others hanging out the sides. Everyone was there.

Charlie's mouth quirked up at the sides. "Ready."

Charlie and Emily climbed aboard. He gave the kids the instructions to all yell out their own street addresses, so that the sleigh would take them home. Rose handed Henry the vial to pour the thick liquid into the spout.

Charlie hugged his sister close.

"Alright, everyone," Charlie yelled. "Here we go. One. Two. Thre—"

"STOP!"

Santa's thunderous voice rebounded through the cave.

Every head snapped over to the entryway. Charlie gripped the sides of the sleigh railing. This wasn't possible.

Scraped, raw, and missing half a horn, Santa stood with his feet planted, and a deadly expression on his face. Behind him, the reindeer guards trotted in with Rudolph, with his swollen eyes and patches of missing fur, followed by all of the elves—including the eight that Charlie was sure fell to their demise just minutes ago.

How?

How could they all be here? How were they all alive? Was it magic?

Charlie stiffened, then inwardly groaned. No, it's because he was *Santa Claus.*

"Surround them," Santa said.

The guards clomped over, eyes narrowed, trotting over like soldiers, surrounding the sleigh. The kids slouched, some has tears in their eyes.

"Your plan has failed," Santa said to Charlie. "*No one* will be going home. All of these naughty children will be going back to the mines. I hope you enjoyed your moment of victory while it lasted."

The kids slowly filed out of the sleigh. With their heads dropped and faces solemn, they marched toward the entrance where Santa stood. The reindeer lined on either side of them, whips at the ready, eyes watchful, as Blitzen motioned them from the cave.

Wind whipped through the tunnel's entrance, whistling and howling. Goosebumps tickled along Charlie's neck, spreading across his back. He stood frozen, staring at the defeated kids, and at Santa's satisfied smirk—that looked so much like his own.

"Wait," Charlie said, though it came out in a whisper.

"Wait—" Charlie tried again.

The kids continued to march, their eyes glued to their feet.

"Wait!" Charlie yelled.

Finally, the room turned.

Charlie stepped forward, looking Santa directly in the eye. "Don't you think you should check your Naughty and Nice book?"

Santa squished his face inward, his coarse lips pressing together tight.

"Check it," Charlie said. "Check it, and you'll see that everyone *will* be going home tonight."

Santa kept his eyes locked with Charlie's. The cave stayed silent. Without moving his gaze, Santa threw his arm out to the side.

"Blitzen!" he ordered. "The book. Now!"

Blitzen galloped to Santa's warehouse and returned, with the book tucked neatly under his arm. He brushed by Charlie, glaring, until he set the book in Santa's hands.

Santa flipped the book open. He ran through the pages, scanning them, until he stopped on the Nice List. He dragged his finger down the page until his eyebrows raised, and a chuckle escaped his mouth.

"So... you've written everyone's name on the Nice List, have you?" His laugh deepened. "You really think that you can get away with this trick twice?"

Santa flipped to the back of the book, and the old man shook his head. The pages crinkled, and Charlie knew he was scanning the Naughty List. He held his breath.

"No new names on the Naughty List..." Santa mumbled, still turning the pages. He lifted his head. "My boy, I'm quite disappointed in you. Did you honestly not learn the last time you tried to fool me?"

Santa continued to turn the pages. His brows shot up, before they pressed over his eyes, and he squinted.

"You left something here," he said. "I can't quite..."

Santa paled. "What is this?"

"Go ahead," Charlie said. "Why don't you tell everyone what you see."

Santa's eyes protruded, the deep red veins matching the heat crawling up his neck.

"No? Nothing?" Charlie asked. "Then let me tell them." Charlie addressed the group. "There's only one name on the Permanent Naughty list. And it's *Charlie Peters*."

The room stilled.

Every eye looked in Charlie's direction.

"No!" Emily cried.

Santa lowered the book. He rubbed his coal-blackened beard. "And why, my boy, would you do such a thing?"

Charlie took a few steps forward, moving into the middle of the cave.

"I've been a naughty kid all my life," he said. "Naughty to my parents, my teachers, my friends, and… my little sister." He glanced over at Emily, who had tears gathering in her eyes. "I deserve this punishment. My sister, she doesn't. She's been nothing but good. Her whole life she's been nice to everybody. Emily doesn't deserve to be here. She even defended me when I *didn't* deserve to be defended. She's here because of my own selfishness." Charlie hefted out a sigh. "Emily, Santa was right. It is my fault you're here. I'm so sorry. I'm so sorry for all of the terrible things I've done to you over the years. You didn't deserve it"

Charlie swallowed the lump in his throat.

"And you guys." Charlie motioned to Rose, Henry and Zach, and the rest of the kids lined up by the door.

"They all deserve to go home, too," he said to Santa. "They've worked hard mining your coal. They've learned their lesson. They earned the right to go home. Even though I got them all in trouble, they risked everything to help me when they didn't have to."

A gust of wind blew in, ruffling Charlie's hair, and Charlie tightened his eyes.

"I will stay on the Permanent List forever if the rest can go home."

Santa linked his arms behind his back. He paced in front of a pile of coal, walking from one end of the cave to the other. Wind continued to whip outside, the sound roaring, chilling straight to Charlie's bones.

"You do realize, that you will never receive Christmas presents ever again, right?" Santa asked.

The pit of Charlie's stomach lurched, but Charlie planted his feet into the ground, and he lifted his chin. "What good are presents to someone who is only nice one month out of the year? Only people who are good all the time deserve them. I don't."

Santa continued to pace, his boots heavy in the dark, his face contorted into a grimace.

"Please," Charlie said. "Just let them go—and I'll report to the mines!"

Santa spun on Charlie and strode toward him. "Is that what you want?"

"Yes!"

A tingle rushed from the top of Charlie's head down to the ends of his toes.

Santa's heavy boots quieted.

Pillars of light streamed into the cave.

The lines in Santa's forehead softened. His stern scowl morphed into a genuine smile. His brown coat with splotches of dirt and grime gave way to a velvety red and white. His chapped cheeks smoothed out into a rosy pink. The bits of crumbs and soot dissipated, revealing a snowy, white beard. His blood-shot eyes cleared into a twinkle.

Charlie rubbed his eyes and glanced around.

The world blurred in the corners of his vision. The ground

shifted under his feet, and Charlie gripped the sides of his head. Charlie spun around, eyes wide. The cave seemed to be melting… the shapes and sounds morphing around him. The rocky cave misted away, the stone walls slowly changing into green and red striped wallpaper, the large boulders dissolving into tasseled pillows and cozy armchairs, and an old, blackened log transforming into a crackling fire in a fireplace.

Charlie blinked.

What?

The gaping hole in the cave wall was a window with laced curtains, revealing snowflakes falling quietly to the ground. The sleigh was now a shining crimson, no longer a corroded metal, with paint peeling on its surface. Instead of the rusted trimming, polished, golden bars swirled around the fresh-coated paint, flames from the fire reflecting off the shiny surface.

An entire wall dissolved away revealing Santa's warehouse. The piles of coal turned into piles of toys, and the conveyor spit out neatly wrapped gifts instead of black rock.

The reindeer guard morphed and transfigured, their bodies twisting up and down, until they were regular reindeer, standing quietly off to one side. Even Rudolph, sat on a knit blanket, with his glowing

227

nose, snuggled up next to an armchair.

The children lined up by the door melted into smaller sized versions of themselves, their faces evolving, becoming elf-like, ears elongating and pointing. They each turned and smiled softly at Charlie, their cheeks a brushed pink. Their clothes became pressed and clean— their once dirty feet now covered in pointed leather shoes, with polished jingle bells resonating in harmony.

One elf exploded from the crowd, jumping up and down. He had a large gap in between his two front teeth.

"Can you believe it? Huh? Huh Huh? I've been waiting so long I couldn't contain myself! Gosh, I've been bursting to tell you everything! It feels so good to use my voice again. Let's start from the beginning. And it feels so good to be back in my own skin again." He ran his tiny hands over his finely stitched silk green shirt.

Charlie jerked back, his eyes bugging wide. "H—Henry? You can… talk?"

An elf with auburn hair and a beauty mark by her eye marched up. "Henry's a bit of a blabber mouth." She punched Henry in the arm. "We had to magically take away his voice. Otherwise he would've spoiled everything."

"Rose?" Charlie said, in disbelief.

Another elf strode up. He had freckles spattered all over his face.

"Zach?" Charlie asked. "Is that really you?"

"Give me a glass of milk and I'll prove it," he joked, rubbing his stomach.

Santa moved across the room and set a kind hand on Charlie's shoulder. He gently drew Charlie to the fireplace and warmed his hands over the snapping flames.

"You only saw us the way you *wanted* to see us in your head, Charlie," Santa explained, his snowy white beard glowing in the dancing light. "But now, you see us the way you *needed* to see us… in your heart."

Charlie moved up next to him, watching as Santa turned the crisp, white pages of the Naughty and Nice Book. Using the magic of his finger, Santa added, *Charlie Peters* onto the Nice List.

"I believe you can go home." Santa winked.

Charlie stopped. The fire crackled, and his heart pounded in his chest.

"I… I think I would like that." Charlie released a long breath.

Charlie soaked in the scene before him. His gaze caught

Blitzen's, who gave him a single nod.

"Santa," Charlie started, "Merry Christmas." He hugged Santa around his big belly. And to his surprise, it actually jiggled like a bowl-full of jelly.

Santa's rosy cheeks brightened, and his eyes twinkled. "Merry Christmas, Chester McScrooge." He laid a finger aside his nose.

Charlie's eyes popped open. He was lying in his bed. The morning light peeked in from the edges of the window shade.

Charlie sat upright.

And gasped.

23.

I sprang from my bed to see what was the matter…

Charlie leapt out of bed and rushed over to the window. He yanked up the shades, and beams of morning light blinded his eyes. A thick layer of snow bent the pine branches, the fresh blanket glistening along rooftops, sidewalks, and treetops, making the whole scene look like a giant, glittering marshmallow.

Charlie blinked, unable to breath. He'd never noticed how beautiful the snow was before. It was fun for snowball fights, but the way the sunlight hit the surface, making the tops look like diamonds, took his breath away. He opened the window with a creak, and the crisp air filled his nose. Old fall leaves mingled with frozen water hit his senses, as the moist air reddened his cheeks. The quiet sounds of winter were like music to his ears, and Charlie watched as a plop of heavy snow fell from a tree branch.

Charlie took in the scene, wondering what day it was.

He jerked.

The date!

Charlie dashed to his computer and started it up.

December Twenty-Fifth.

7:05 a.m.

Charlie fell back into his desk chair, scratching the top of his bushy head. He didn't know how this was possible. Although he felt like he'd been gone for days, he'd only gone for a few hours. Maybe it had been just a dream—but it couldn't have been. It had all been too real.

Emily.

Charlie jumped from his seat and bolted from the room and down the hall to his sister's doorway. He threw open the door, eyes darting around the space. Her small form lay in bed, her face relaxed into sleep. Charlie's heart slowed and his shoulders loosened. He didn't realize how worried he was that she'd be gone.

Charlie crept across the room. He sat on the edge of her bed.

"Emily," he said, gently nudging her shoulder. "Emily, wake up."

Her eyelids fluttered, and she peeked open.

"Hey," he said. "It's Christmas morning."

She sat up in a rush, bouncing on the bed, her mouth stretching wide. Charlie's heart tugged, and he never wanted to make that smile disappear again. Charlie grabbed his sister and gave her a hug to make up for all the years he hadn't.

Emily pushed away slightly.

"Uh, who are you and what have you done with my brother?"

Charlie only smiled and hugged her some more.

Finally, Emily clapped her hands. "Let's go wake Mom and Dad!"

Charlie laughed as he joined Emily in her excitement. For the first time, his heart soared as he ran to his parents' bedroom, happy because Emily was happy... and joyful because he was with his family.

"Wake up! Wake up! It's Christmas morning!" Emily yelled.

Charlie's parents yawned as they trudged out of bed in their matching flannel pajamas, their hair mussed to the sides.

"Let's go open presents!" Emily squealed. "I wonder what Santa brought me!"

Emily leapt down the stairs two at a time and his parents followed.

Charlie's foot hovered over the first step. He didn't know if there would be any presents for him. All of the name tags could say Emily. It could be too late for someone like him. He'd been so horrible up to this point in his life, it was probably too late to make it up.

Charlie peered down the stairs, he couldn't see anything, but he could hear Emily's laughter.

Presents didn't matter, he reminded himself—just being with his family made him happy—seeing Emily smile was happiness in and of itself. Though Charlie's throat swelled, and his stomach twisted.

There was only one way to find out.

24

It's beginning to look a lot like Christmas…

Charlie entered the living room, and the scene before him exploded to life.

Lights. Presents. Tinsel. Stockings. The ornaments on the tree glowed as the Christmas lights gleamed, changing color. Dad's toy train ran around the bottom of the tree, choo-choo-ing, and Christmas music played from Mom's old record player. Bright green, red, and white presents loaded the entire area, curled bows and ribbons around each one. Candy canes and wrapped chocolates had been scattered throughout the room, like Santa's elves had had a candy fight.

Charlie's parents sat collapsed on the couch, watching as Emily darted from present to present picking up each box and shaking them.

"Charlie! I wonder what this one could be! Do you think it's the Barbie doll I've been asking for?"

Charlie's mouth pushed up to one side. "I don't know. We better open it and see. But let's count how many presents you got first!"

Emily's eyes lit up as they bent underneath the tree, carefully admiring each gift. Emily counted under her breath, her smile growing broader, her face full of wonder.

Charlie piled up the presents for Emily, finding each one with her name on it, but the further he dug through the pile, the more his heart sunk. One after another, he found Emily's name. He didn't find his own. Maybe it was too late. Maybe he hadn't been good enough this year. Maybe he hadn't learned his lesson in time. Maybe—

"Charlie!" Emily squealed.

Charlie's head shot up.

"This one's for you!" Emily skipped over and handed Charlie a red and white striped package, with a crisp, white bow on top. "Merry Christmas, Charlie!"

Charlie accepted the gift, the wrapping paper cool and smooth under his fingertips. His chest squeezed as he turned the box over in his hands.

"Aren't you going to open it?" Emily asked.

"Oh, um. Sure. But here, I found another one for you." Charlie picked up a sparkling white present and handed it to his sister.

"Thanks."

The siblings eyed each other for a moment and smiles slowly spread over their faces. Their hands gripped their presents, fingers inching upward, nails pulling at the corners, before chaos broke loose.

Wrapping paper flew from all directions.

Charlie's parents sighed as they watched the cacophony of paper and bows fly upward.

It was over in seconds.

Charlie sat back, lying in the pile of paper.

"Santa sure has been good to us this year," he said.

Emily set her new doll down, her forehead crinkled. "I thought you didn't believe in Santa."

Charlie sat up and set his hands on his knees. "I do." His mouth pulled in and he dropped his gaze. "You showed me that he's real, Emily." Charlie looked at her directly. "Thank you."

Emily's eyes shone as she grinned. "Again, I don't know who you are, but I like the new you."

"Who wants gingerbread?" Charlie's mother asked, stepping into the room. She carried a tray and lowered it in front of Charlie's face. The spicy smell tingled his nose.

Charlie glanced between Emily and the tray. Emily clasped her hands together, batting her eyes.

"Come on, Charlie. Try my Rudolph one!"

Charlie snatched the cookie with the cheerful dotted eyes and mouth, and the red frosted nose. Charlie tentatively took a bite. He chewed and swallowed.

"It's not *so* bad."

It was actually kind of good.

"It's good to give things a second chance," Charlie's mother said. "Speaking of which." Her eyes flicked downward.

Fluffy scampered in and rubbed her body against Charlie's leg. Charlie froze, staring at the furry beast. The cat continued to nestle in. Finally, Charlie reached down and scratched its head. The cat purred and snuggled into Charlie's hand.

"Charlie, want to play with me?" Emily bounced on her tippy-toes, shoving her new doll in his face.

Charlie jumped to his feet, grabbing his new action figure. "You know it!"

Charlie's parents stared at each other, dazed. They watched Charlie play with his little sister for the very first time. Normally, he would have cut the doll's hair off by now and removed her limbs. They sensed a change in him. Even Fluffy could sense it. Somehow, they knew their son would no longer be naughty.

They knew he would be nice.

All year round.

"Oh!" his mother exclaimed, her hand flying to her mouth. "We forgot the stockings!"

25

And to all a good night.

Emily dumped out her stocking, revealing an assortment of candies and sweets, along with a few more individually wrapped gifts. She sat at the base of the fireplace, lining the goodies up by color and size, her blonde curls covering her face.

Charlie stared down his own stocking, his feet rooted to the floor.

He zoomed in on the green and red knitting, where his name was stitched in white, then down to the toe, where it hung heavy, wondering what lay inside. His heart skipped and skidded, then quivered in his chest. The world seemed to blur on either side of him. All he could see was the thick wool sock, the stocking appearing to grow the longer he stood there.

Charlie slowly took a step forward. Then another. And another. In the back of his mind, he could hear Emily squealing with delight, he could hear his parent's sighing with relief—but their voices were muted, as his focus was on one thing.

The stocking.

Charlie's hand reached forward and removed the stocking from off the mantel. His hand dropped from the weight of the sock. Something was in there.

He pulled in a deep breath.

Inside, the stocking was soft and warm, fuzzy and smooth. Charlie's hand slid downward. He clenched his eyes shut, expecting to feel the cold, hard, craggy surface of a lump of coal. Instead, Charlie's fingers hit a flat, square box. His eyes snapped open, and he pulled it out.

With his eyebrows pressed together, he unlatched the box and lifted the lid. He tilted his head.

Inside, cradled in a pillow of velvet, was a small, clear glass sphere. Veins of orange and red swirled with a hint of black. Charlie's hand hovered over the globe, his heart leaping, his breath trapped in his throat. Charlie reached inside and picked up the marble, turning it over in his hands. Light from the window shone through the glass orb, and he admired the way the light played off of the colors.

A Cat's Eye.

So rare.

He'd always wanted one of these.

His fingers trembled as he held the marble close to his chest.

It was the best present he'd ever received.

Charlie noticed a small tag on the inside of that box that read: Make a Wish. He smiled at the possibilities.

Charlie glanced out the window, where fluffy snowflakes had started to fall, the different shapes and patterns sticking to the windowpane. He peered over at the pile of unwrapped gifts, surrounding the tree, where the lights swirled on the ceiling. He smiled as his parents sat on the couch with their cups of hot cocoa, warming their hands, and his throat constricted at Emily, who danced to the Christmas music over by the fire, hugging her new doll.

This was happiness. This was what mattered.

Charlie's spine tingled as he placed the marble back into the wooden box. He clicked the lid shut and held the container close to his heart, a secret smile on his face. He knew the marble was a reminder of the magic of Santa Claus, a reminder that through this Cautionary Christmas Tale, that I see you when you are sleeping, I know when you're awake, I know if you've been bad or good, so be good for goodness sake.

Made in the USA
Lexington, KY
20 November 2019